MR. DARCY'S STOLEN LOVE

HARRIET KNOWLES

Edited by JW Services

Proofreading by Mystique Editing

ISBN-13:9781978342057

ISBN-10:1978342055

CHAPTER 1

*T*he heavy, wobbly feeling that her legs wouldn't hold her up caused Elizabeth to hold more tightly to the edge of the door frame. She wondered sadly how long she would feel like this and immediately felt remorse that she wished to feel better.

Papa was dead. She never wanted to feel his loss any less, or she might stop thinking about him and then he'd be gone forever.

She licked her dry lips. She knew she must look terrible, her face still swollen from three days of weeping. Today would be the hardest day of her life, she thought. Today he would be laid to rest and she could not be there to say goodbye.

She hadn't been there to help him three days ago, either. She and Jane had been walking in the

1

garden, enjoying the sunshine, when the house-keeper had come hastening to them.

"Come quickly, Miss Bennet, come quickly!"

"What is the matter, Hill?" Elizabeth had not felt dread then, but more annoyance for her mother, whose regular bouts of hysteria made her sigh.

"It is your father, please hurry."

Then the dread had fallen on her like a cloak and she had lived with it daily since then.

Her father was dead, his apoplectic seizure showing in the shocked expression frozen on his face. He had fallen back in his chair, his book lying in his lap.

Elizabeth had dropped to her knees beside him, as Jane had sent for the doctor, and Kitty and the staff had struggled to deal with her mother, who was more concerned with her future than the loss of her life companion. Elizabeth had known she needed to stay away, far away from her mother, until she could control her own emotions better.

They had spent three days in the house now, her father laid out in his library and Elizabeth, or occasionally Jane, sitting with him, as the towns-people came to pay their respects. The windows were closed, the curtains too, as they mourned.

Elizabeth felt stifled, she knew she needed to get out of the house and up to the hills.

But it was not the right thing to do when mourning, and she would do what was right for her father. That was the least thing she could do for him — and the last thing, because ladies could not go to the graveside.

Inside, she raged at the thought that strangers would take that journey with him and she couldn't. The strain rose within her as the Collinses arrived, expecting to stay at what was now their estate. But realising the state of things, they decided to stay at Lucas Lodge with Charlotte's parents until after the funeral.

And Mr. Collins would speak at the burial. Elizabeth could do nothing about it, although she spoke to the vicar, expressing her outrage. He smiled sadly, not willing to make a stand for what she thought was right, not wishing to make an enemy of Mr. Collins over Elizabeth, who was now likely to leave the parish. After all, he knew Mr. Collins had powerful patronage.

It was fortunate that Elizabeth had the Gardiners to speak to. They had hurried down and stayed at the local inn, having left their children with the nursemaids in London. Mrs. Gardiner took Elizabeth up to her bedroom and

3

sat with her for many hours, listening to her outpourings of sorrow and anger.

"Elizabeth, dear, you must not tax yourself so. You have difficult times ahead, and you need to stay very strong. Your father would not want you not to be able to think clearly about what is to be done."

Elizabeth shook her head. "There is nothing that can be done. Mr. Collins has inherited the estate, we have nowhere to go."

"Yes, dear. But you cannot allow your thinking to remain like that. Your mother has a small income, you could help her find a cottage to rent here in Meryton and there should just be room for Kitty and Mary to stay with her. You and Jane might wish to come to London with us until you have decided what to do."

Elizabeth glanced at her. "You are very kind, Aunt Gardiner. But I think Mama does not want to stay in Meryton where she will have to watch Mr. and Mrs. Collins at Longbourn." She made a face. "I think she was expecting to go to London."

Mrs. Gardiner was unable to completely mask the expression of distaste which crossed her face. "I understand, and it may come to that. But Mr. Gardiner and I feel very much that she should stay here for the time being and show that she is made of stronger stuff than she actually feels herself to be."

Elizabeth felt a sense of relief. She'd been dreading moving somewhere new, somewhere with no memories of her father and with her mother complaining constantly about his failure to make provision for them. At least the Gardiner's home was familiar to her, and she loved them with all her heart.

"Thank you, I'm most grateful for your invitation. I do have to find something that I can do, though, some way to make a living for myself." Elizabeth hated the thought that her father's death had changed her life in every aspect, when all she wanted to do was have the world stop while she said her goodbyes and let the changes happen gradually. But it could never be.

And now she was standing at the door, as men came to take her father's earthly body on its last journey. She felt cold and sorrow creeping over her. She heard the grunts as the men lifted the coffin onto their shoulders and the wails of her mother and sisters. She could no longer cry.

Stony-faced, she watched as they made their way past her.

Stony-faced, she watched as they loaded the coffin onto the open cart.

Stony-faced, she watched her father leave her forever.

All the women crowded at the doorway as the cortege left the house. Aunt Gardiner stepped back and spoke to the housekeeper, who was waiting for instructions, her own eyes reddened with weeping. Elizabeth realised she could do nothing to help the staff, who all had their own uncertain futures to worry about.

As the woman returned with the maids, bearing a tray of tea and one of cakes and pastries, Elizabeth had had enough. She hurried up to her room, and took up her bonnet, covered with black crepe. She was going out, whatever the niceties demanded. She was going to leave the house, and watch the service from afar. No one could stop her.

"Lizzy! Where are you going? You bad, wicked girl. I need you here with me!" Her mother's querulous voice rose as she returned back through the hall, and Jane came to the door.

"Dear Lizzy, please don't go out. It seems disrespectful."

"Dearest Jane. I must respect my father in my own way. It is wrong that I cannot go to the church. I can at least watch from afar." Elizabeth embraced her sister, and stepped lightly outside.

CHAPTER 2

*S*he drew a great deep breath in gratitude at finally being outside. Father had loved the outdoors when she was a child. It was only in the last few years that he had retired back to his library as his place of security.

She needed to hurry, and she crossed the lane and hastened along the path towards the village church. She thought back to her childhood, when she would skip beside her father when they walked to Meryton to buy some sweetmeats for her, or a new book for his library.

At last she could think of him as he was, and not the memory of her last look at him, his features congested in death. She shuddered and dragged her thoughts back to happier times.

Soon she was standing at the edge of the

woods, half-hidden on the path, and overlooking the churchyard. Her father's coffin lay beside the open grave, and a crowd of men stood by.

She could see Mr. Collins, clerical robes billowing, standing beside the vicar, who held his prayer book open. She could see Uncle Gardiner, and her heart warmed at the sight of him doing his duty to his brother-in-law. There were other familiar people from the village. She saw Sir William Lucas, and wondered if he was gloating over the fact that his daughter would now be mistress of Longbourn.

Then her heart constricted in her throat and she saw Mr. Bingley and Mr. Darcy standing a short way apart from the other men. Both were still, their heads bowed in respect. Elizabeth's own opinion of them improved.

She and Jane had each received a short, terse note of condolence from them, and she had wondered sadly if Jane's chance with Mr. Bingley was now gone, or if he might perhaps return to London to see her.

As for her own view of Mr. Darcy, she knew that she respected him for doing everything properly, keeping the proprieties. But love him? She didn't know. She wanted to be strong, she didn't want to marry just to gain security.

But as she stood there, the temptation stole

over her. It would be nice to wake in the mornings knowing that she would never want for anything ever again, never have to worry about having nowhere to go.

She emptied her mind and watched as the service proceeded. Then the pallbearers lowered her father's coffin into the grave. One by one, the men lined up and sprinkled a handful of earth on top of it.

Standing around the grave, they then stood, heads bowed again, as the vicar, the wind whipping out his robes, read from his prayer book.

She let the tears run down her face. This was it, her final goodbye. She was angry that she could not hear anything, angry that, as a woman, she could not be there.

She understood why her mother disliked her. As a second daughter, she was not welcome. Jane, as the first child, had been. A daughter was nice for a lady to have. But a second daughter — no. A son was needed to secure the inheritance and a second daughter was a disappointment.

And Elizabeth knew that was why her closeness to her father had been so special. He had not let the disappointment show. He had even favoured her, her acute mind and her quick-witted thoughts amusing him and making him laugh.

"Goodbye, Father," she whispered to herself as

the vicar closed his prayer book and made the sign of the cross over the grave. The congregation looked as if they wanted to turn away now, but Mr. Collins stepped forward and began to speak, and rigid correctness kept them all there.

Mr. Darcy was standing stock still, but he looked up, and he saw Elizabeth. They stared at each other for a long moment, then he bowed his head slightly and kept his gaze away. Perhaps he didn't want to draw attention to her presence there, or perhaps he disapproved of her being there at all. Either way, Elizabeth didn't care.

She waited the age that Mr. Collins exhorted them, seeing them beginning to shift from foot to foot, and then she watched as Mr. Darcy nudged Mr. Bingley and the two men turned and walked away, in an act of calculated rudeness that made Elizabeth's lips curve in the first smile since her father's death.

Mr. Bennet would have approved of that. In fact, had he been there, he would have walked away too. She sniffed, and watched as the rest of the crowd gave up and followed the gentlemen away.

The only people left were Mr. Gardiner, Sir William Lucas and the vicar, and Mr. Collins stopped and looked around. Elizabeth thought that her uncle must have a favour to ask of Mr.

Collins. That would be the only thing that would keep him there. And Sir William would not wish to offend his son-in-law.

She stayed in the shelter of the trees and watched them all leave the churchyard. Then, cold and depressed, she slowly made her way home.

SHE WISHED Lady Catherine de Bourgh would demand that Mr. and Mrs. Collins return to Hunsford until she had found a new man to fill the vacancy. Then they might have time to look around for a cottage for her mother. But she thought dismally that they wouldn't do that. They would want the family out, and take great delight in altering the property to suit themselves.

No. She needed to be far away from Longbourn. Far, far away. As she returned to the house, she could hear much wailing from her mother. She slipped in quietly and went upstairs to her room. The house seemed very empty.

After a few minutes sitting quietly, she sighed. It would not do to leave Jane having to manage the family alone, and she trod heavily down the stairs.

The reason for all the noise was soon communicated to her. A letter had been delivered to Mrs. Bennet not long after the coffin had left the house. Mr. Collins must have written it prior to going to the church and also arranged for it to be delivered during the funeral.

In his usual overblown and effusive language, he enquired where the family were going to be living in future, in order to redirect any correspondences that might be received after they had left the house. There was no indication that any extra time was to be given them.

Mrs. Gardiner and Jane called Elizabeth over to them. It was perfectly plain to her that no help or reason was to be obtained from her mother or sisters.

"So what has happened since you got the letter?" Elizabeth asked.

"About what you expected," sighed Jane. "Mama said that she expected Uncle Gardiner to arrange the coach to London and Aunt Gardiner asked then what Mama intended to do with all her belongings in that instance, reminding her that there is not enough room in Gracechurch Street to take very much. Since then, Mama has been inconsolable."

"Oh, that is a great pity." Elizabeth had thought of something and looked towards her mother.

"Mama, I have been thinking. If we find a place for you to live near here, then you will be able to continually remind all the local families of Mr. Collins' unreasonable and unChristian behaviour." Her mother suddenly became quiet and really listened. Elizabeth continued. "We could find a cottage quite close to Aunt Philips and they will have some secure place for the belongings you cannot bear to part with."

"Oh, Lizzy, that is such a wicked suggestion," Jane murmured as Mrs. Bennet loudly considered the proposal.

Elizabeth smiled sadly. "It is exactly the sort of thing that Papa would have thought of."

They all sat quiet at that, but in no time at all, the plan seemed to be quite approved of, and Aunt Gardiner said that she and Mr. Gardiner would go and see Mr. and Mrs. Philips immediately when he returned to the house and they would procure somewhere appropriate. She did not mention the word affordable in front of Mrs. Bennet.

Mrs. Bennet, encouraged into action by the thought of being able to be a thorn in the side of the odious Mr. Collins, heaved herself to her feet and went into the hall, calling the staff.

"Hill! Hill, where are you? Come along, get

everyone starting to pack away our things! We have to get along and get ourselves ready to go!"

Jane and Elizabeth were left sitting staring at each other.

"What have we done?" Jane shook her head. "I do not imagine Aunt Philips will be happy that Mama is remaining in Meryton."

"No," said Elizabeth. "However, I do not think it is good for the young Gardiner children if she were to be in London, either."

Jane could not contest her sister's comment and together they got wearily to their feet and went out to see how they could assist in the plans.

CHAPTER 3

No sooner had the house descended into complete disarray than Kitty came rushing downstairs, calling that she could see Mr. Bingley and Mr. Darcy in a chaise turning into the drive.

"Oh, my goodness!" Jane became quite pink and Elizabeth turned and smiled at her.

"It is not a difficulty, Jane, the parlour is still quite suitable for you to entertain Mr. Bingley. And you must." She drew her sister into her bedroom. "But first, we must make sure you look suitably in mourning. Such respect is expected." She carefully tidied her sister's hair and made sure her clothing was neat and tidy. They had black fabric sewn onto their plainest dresses as a mark of mourning, there not being the money to buy black clothing.

Then the sisters descended the stairs. Mrs. Bennet was flustered upstairs still.

"No, Mama, you must not be seen today." Elizabeth was firm. "Aunt Gardiner will chaperone us."

"And why must I not be seen?" Mrs. Bennet began to work herself up into an attack of hysterics.

"Because your nerves are affected, and you are still in close mourning." Elizabeth was quite decided that she was going to prevail in this confrontation, she knew that her mother might say something that would be quite wrong.

But why the gentlemen had in fact arrived the same day as the funeral, she could not imagine.

She and Jane turned into the parlour to join their sisters and Mrs. Gardiner, and the two men who were standing by the fireplace turned and bowed. Mr. Darcy was his usual enigmatic self, but Mr. Bingley looked pink and embarrassed.

He bent over Jane's hand. "Oh, Miss Bennet, I am so sorry for your grievous loss."

She murmured a reply and sat down. Elizabeth sat beside her, and the two gentlemen stood stiffly opposite, declining to be seated.

After a moment Mrs. Gardiner gathered her needlework. "Come along, Mary, come along, Kitty. We have plenty of work to do upstairs." She shepherded them out of the room.

There was a silence in the room for a few moments. Elizabeth sat with her gaze on her hands resting in her lap.

Neither of the Bennet sisters began a subject, it was not seemly. But Mr. Bingley also did not know what to say. He shifted from foot to foot, clearing his throat occasionally.

Mr. Darcy stepped forward slightly. "I am sorry, Miss Bennet, and Miss Elizabeth Bennet, that we have called on you so soon. I am aware of the fact that it is most unseemly to disturb you this early in your period of mourning, and we would not normally wish to disturb you thus."

He hesitated. "But when Mr. Collins spoke at the funeral, we became aware that he seems to expect that he and Mrs. Collins will be moving into this house without delay and we have heard nothing that comforted us with the knowledge that you had settled plans." He waited a moment or two, as if hoping he could be reassured and thus make his escape without having to do very much.

But there was nothing to say. Elizabeth kept her head down, she would not let him see how very much her father's death had affected her, and more, that he had made no provision for them.

Jane lifted her head proudly. "Thank you for your concern, I appreciate your thoughtfulness." She was looking at Mr. Bingley rather than Mr. Darcy.

"I am sure something is to be thought of, but first we are proposing that Mr. Gardiner procure a small home for our mother and our two younger sisters. Mother has a small settlement of her own that will suffice. We hope they can find somewhere close to Mrs Philips in Meryton, who is, of course, related to her."

She turned to Elizabeth. "It has been suggested that Lizzy and I go to London, to stay with our aunt and uncle, at least at first."

Mr. Bingley seemed a little taken aback, but he took a deep breath. Elizabeth realised he had something to say and he was determined to say it.

"Miss Bennet," he said, and hesitated again. "Miss Bennet. I know that it seems so much an inauspicious moment to make these suggestions to you. But, as Mr. Darcy says, circumstances compel me to assure myself of your safety and security without delay. I wish to invite you to Netherfield where you may stay as long as you wish. Of course, my sister is resident there to provide you with a suitable chaperone, so your honour would be preserved. And, of course, Miss Elizabeth is most welcome too. You will be able to be close by and see your mother settled, and then … and then, make other plans for the future when you are finished with mourning." He stopped, his expression transparent to Elizabeth.

She knew that had it been correct, he would have proposed to Jane that very moment, and she knew that he would do so the moment she was out of mourning.

Jane was looking stunned and amazed. "Why, Mr. Bingley, that is a most generous offer, I hardly know how to respond." She turned to Elizabeth, her eyes shining for the first time since Mr. Bennet's death, and Elizabeth was comforted a little.

She turned to Mr. Bingley. "It is a most kind offer, sir. I wonder if my sister and I might have a few moments to discuss it?"

The men bowed to her, and Mr. Darcy spoke for them both.

"Of course. Perhaps we might wait in the gardens a moment." They left the room, and Elizabeth turned to Jane the moment she saw their figures outside the front door.

"Oh, Jane, that is so kind of him, is it not?"

Jane looked quite animated. "Yes, it is. But of

course I — we — must refuse. It would seem most imprudent to accept."

"I do not agree." Elizabeth thought the idea was splendid for Jane. "It would be most impolite to refuse him and I am sure that he would propose marriage this moment if propriety allowed it. To go and stay with him until mourning is over will give you much happiness and it will give you security, too." She smiled at her sister. "We can plan your wedding in the greatest of detail."

"But you will not come with me." Jane knew her sister very well.

"No, I will not. But not because of the proprieties. It is because I cannot live for long in the same house as Miss Caroline Bingley. However, she likes you and is most agreeable to you."

Jane shook her head. "It is better that you and I stay in London together in that case. Perhaps Mr. Bingley will open his London residence."

"No, Jane. Stay here. Mr. Bingley is much more available to dance attendance upon you than he might be in London. After all, Cheapside is the wrong side of town for Caroline." She smiled archly at her sister. "And, after all, it will be good for me to know that you can supervise Mary and Kitty learning to manage Mama by themselves."

Jane nodded thoughtfully. "I suppose you are

right." She looked up with an untroubled smile on her face. "And I am sure you will ask to take up the invitation if Mama does go to London."

"You are improper to think such a thing of me, Jane." Elizabeth could feel herself beginning to smile. It seemed that knowing her sister could be secure had helped her a little in coming to accept the loss of her father.

"Will you go outside and tell them, Lizzy?" Jane rose to her feet. "I think I will blush with embarrassment at accepting his offer."

"I will do that with much pleasure on your behalf, Jane." Elizabeth got to her feet as well. "You might go and tell Mama. But only once the gentlemen have gone."

She slipped outside the house to where the men were standing waiting. Mr. Darcy stood still as a statue, gazing out over the landscape. Mr. Bingley was fidgeting a little, watching the door. She wondered again at the differences between the two men and how they found themselves friends.

Mr. Bingley hurried towards her as she came through the door and Mr. Darcy moved closer to listen, too.

She curtsied. "Mr. Bingley, my sister thanks you for your most kind thoughtfulness and attention to her. She is very grateful for your generous offer and hopes that she might accept it."

"Oh, that is tremendously good news." He seemed joyful and disbelieving at his good fortune at the same time. "I am happy at your persuasions on my behalf, for I know she values your opinions greatly. And will you accompany your sister? You are most welcome."

She shook her head. "You are exceptionally kind and generous, sir. But I must decline your offer. I trust most sincerely your goodwill towards Jane and believe she will be safe with you." She curtsied again and saw him glance at Mr. Darcy, rather discomfited.

That gentleman looked sharply at her, then spoke to his friend.

"Bingley, of your favour, might you wait a moment at the chaise? I wish to speak to Miss Bennet."

When that gentleman had repaired to wait by the chaise, Mr. Darcy moved closer to Elizabeth. "I am most sorry that you do not feel able to remain a companion to your sister. At this time of grief, you could be of great comfort to each other."

She looked up at him, rather surprised, because she had not thought him capable of such consideration to others, especially to those ladies he considered beneath him.

"I thank you for your concern, sir, but you need not heed it. My desire is to leave the neighbourhood of Longbourn and Meryton and the invitation of my aunt and uncle affords me the means by which to do so."

He nodded slowly. "So, I am surprised that you do not wish your sister to accompany you, that being the case."

"You do not need to concern yourself with this matter, as I have said, sir. Above all else, I wish my sister to be happy, and, given the circumstances of the offer, I believe that she will be happiest here, in the company at Netherfield, and close to such family as remains." Her chin went up.

"We have reason to be grateful to you, sir, for the efforts you made to ensure the actions of Lydia did not stain our family. But that does not mean we are in need of your assistance now."

He looked at her for a moment. "On the contrary, Miss Bennet, I remain concerned on your behalf. A lady is very open to becoming in dire circumstances should the male members of the family not be able to apportion adequate allowance for her, and I would not like you to think you had no recourse to any security."

He hesitated. "If you wish to leave this locality, Pemberley is a good distance away, as you know. My young sister, Georgiana, would welcome a companion should you feel the need for some occupation." His face was strained. "And, of course, there would be no time limit to your stay there. It would be until you felt able to make decisions yourself as to your future."

Elizabeth stepped back, and took a very deep breath. "No. No, sir. I ... thank you for the offer, which I am sure was nobly meant, but you cannot give out an invitation of that nature. What if you should marry? Your wife would find it most unseemly to have a young woman of my background chosen as a companion to your sister."

His features darkened and she wondered what he was thinking. Perhaps he was imagining Miss Caroline Bingley as his wife and what she should think. Elizabeth almost laughed at the thought of running away from Netherfield because of Miss Caroline Bingley and then finding herself at Pemberley and Miss Bingley as the new Mrs. Darcy.

He was watching her. "So, where will you go?"

"I will go to London, sir. Gracechurch Street is familiar to me, and I love my Aunt Gardiner dearly. She will never turn me away." She stepped back. It was time to part from him, and move on with her life away from here.

"Thank you for taking the time to talk to me." He bowed to her. "I expect Mr. Bingley will send the coach to be ready for your sister and her belongings whenever she is ready."

Elizabeth curtsied back. "That is most thoughtful of him. Thank you." And she turned and walked back towards the house.

CHAPTER 4

*I*t was very late that night when she arrived in London with Mr. and Mrs. Gardiner and they were all exhausted from their efforts in Hertfordshire.

But Mrs. Bennet was securely ensconced in a small cottage in Meryton, leading Kitty and Mary her usual merry dance, with Hill now their only servant.

Jane and her belongings had been packed off to Netherfield Hall in time for dinner, and Elizabeth had wept after it left, having determined to stay brave until her sister was out of sight.

She had little of her own to take with her, but had slipped into her father's library and selected a few of his favourite books, recklessly disregarding that the whole estate belonged to Mr. Collins. She carefully moved a few other books along the shelf, so that the absence of those she had taken would not be remarked upon.

Mrs. Gardiner smiled when she saw it. "What a good idea, Lizzy. They will comfort you wherever you go." She had watched as Elizabeth helped Jane for her move to Netherfield and Elizabeth knew that she was determined to ask why Elizabeth had not gone too. But she also knew that would be for the coach journey back to London.

And that had been the case.

Elizabeth shook her head. "Dear aunt, I know you are curious, and I will tell you. But just tonight I am so tired and weary as to probably render the explanation incomprehensible. I hope you might wait a day or two for a more sensible exposition." And Elizabeth had then laid her head against the window of the coach with her eyes closed, allowing the pain of the loss of her home to mingle with the still-raw absence of her father. And thus she went to London in a stupor of misery.

～

THE HOUSE at Gracechurch Street was commodious and Elizabeth woke late the following morning in the room she had always stayed in. The familiarity comforted her and she brushed her hair in front of the glass feeling a little more hopeful than she had for half a week.

As she thought back to the previous day, she could scarce believe that so much had happened in so short a time. It was all crushed in together in a sharp painful memory. Her father's coffin leaving the house. Watching his burial from afar. Mr. Bingley and Mr. Darcy, making their offers, deciding what was best for them. Finding a place for her mother and moving her in. Saying goodbye to Jane. Saying goodbye to Longbourn in the dark. Driving through the night to London.

Perhaps it was as well that it was all blurred by exhaustion. The pain of the memories would fade that much faster, she hoped. And now she was in London, where she had often stayed alone, or with Jane.

This house was not full of memories of her father and she might be able to remember him with more affection than sorrow sooner than if she had stayed in Hertfordshire.

The bedroom door creaked open, and a few curious little faces peered in. The Gardiner children were calling. Soon the room was full of small bodies tumbling around on her bed like eager puppies, and Elizabeth laughed to see them.

Her heart pained her as she automatically thought to write and tell her father of the scene, but she pushed the thought away.

"Yes, it will hurt like that at odd moments for a long time." Aunt Gardiner came into the room and sat on a chair, watching her niece with sympathy. "But it is good that you do not feel you must not laugh. Your father would want you to be happy, to remember the joyful times."

Elizabeth nodded. "I know. But lately he was not enjoying many of the things he had previously. I wonder now if he knew what was happening."

"It is possible." Her aunt was thoughtful. "But there is no useful purpose to be served by wondering if you could have changed anything had you known."

"Dear Aunt." Elizabeth smiled affectionately at her. "I hope to be helpful to you while I am here, and not a burden. I wish you to tell me when there is anything I can do."

"That I will most certainly do." Mrs. Gardiner smiled as she stood up. "To begin with, it is good that the children feel you are here to entertain them."

TWO DAYS PASSED and Elizabeth filled her room

with her possessions as she unpacked. She told herself that she would be here for the summer at least, and determined to feel settled and at home and not to worry about her future.

After breakfast, she set herself down in the drawing room to write to Jane as she had done each day so far. Today or tomorrow she hoped that she would hear from Jane that all was well with her, and maybe from Kitty or Mary as to how they were progressing.

Mrs. Gardiner was sitting by the window to get better light for her needlework, when the housekeeper knocked at the door and presented her with a calling card.

"Oh!" Mrs. Gardiner sounded surprised. "Mr. Darcy!"

Elizabeth looked up, startled.

"Thank you, Mrs. Peters. You may show him in." Mrs. Gardiner looked over at her niece, her eyebrows raised.

Elizabeth shook her head, puzzled. She had been certain that he would not stoop to calling on them here, in Cheapside.

He entered the room and bowed, first at his hostess, and then toward Elizabeth. Both ladies had risen, and curtsied in return. Then Mrs. Gardiner indicated a chair to him and they all sat.

"Thank you for calling, Mr. Darcy. Is all well

at Netherfield?" Mrs. Gardiner was elegant and amiable, well able to begin the conversation.

Mr. Darcy nodded at her. "Indeed, madam. I thank you for receiving me." His eyes turned towards Elizabeth.

"I wonder, Miss Bennet, if you have had the pleasure of hearing from your sister at Netherfield, yet?"

"No, sir, not yet."

He smiled thinly at her. "Of course, it is very early days, Miss Bennet. However, I have just received an overnight express letter from Mr. Bingley, and since he mentions your sister, I thought it might be appropriate for me to bring it around to you so that you have early news."

Elizabeth's heart jumped into her throat.

"No, no!" he said hastily. "It is good news, Miss Bennet. Please do not distress yourself."

She sagged back in relief.

"It is very kind of you to come straight here, Mr. Darcy." Mrs. Gardiner smoothed her skirts. "We will be very happy to hear the news."

He reached inside his jacket and drew out a few folded sheets of letter paper. He sorted through them. "Here. Here is where he mentions Miss Bennet." He handed Elizabeth the single sheet.

"Thank you," she murmured. She searched

down the lines until she found Jane's name mentioned.

> *It is proving a delight having Miss Jane Bennet staying here, Darcy. I will never be able to thank you enough for your suggestion. The last time she stayed, of course, she was very unwell, but on this occasion, although she is naturally very sad at the loss of her father and her home, she is well, and able to attend dinner with us each night.*
>
> *I managed to persuade her to walk in the gardens this morning, and it was gratifying to see a little colour in her face when she did so.*
>
> *Caroline is being very kind to her, and the two ladies spend much time in each other's company.*
>
> *I hope your business in London proves satisfactory, and remember you are always very welcome here.*

She folded up the letter and handed it back to him. "Thank you for showing it to me, Mr. Darcy. It seems Jane is being exceedingly well looked after."

He bowed to her, and handed the sheet to Mrs. Gardiner, who read it quickly and handed it back to him.

"It was very good of you to think of telling us the news, Mr. Darcy." She rose to her feet. "I will ask the housekeeper to arrange for some refreshment." And she swept from the room, leaving Elizabeth alone with their guest.

A moment's silence ensued and Elizabeth raised her head. "I see Mr. Bingley refers to your business in London, sir. Will it keep you in London for a protracted period?"

He nodded. "I am expecting it to take a while, so I have opened my establishment and will remain here for the time being, although I expect to dine at Netherfield regularly. It is not too far so I am able to contemplate that."

Elizabeth nodded. It was a life she could hardly comprehend. Even at Longbourn, there was always the constraint of having to spare the horses from the farm before one could ascertain the availability of the coach for any sort of journey. Even had she a carriage available for her use, a young, unmarried lady could hardly have the freedom of movement a single gentleman was afforded. And after marriage, a lady's life was constrained by her husband.

Freedom would never be hers and it was something her heart had never repined after, beyond a brief passing fancy.

She noted he was looking at her curiously, and she started.

"I am most sorry, sir. Did you speak? I was thinking of something else."

He smiled, a rather strained smile. "You have much to think about, Miss Bennet. I am intruding." He stood and bowed to her. "Thank you for receiving me."

As he turned and went to the door, Mrs. Gardiner entered.

"Oh, are you leaving us so soon, Mr. Darcy? I hope that all is in order?"

He bowed to her. "Indeed, madam. It was my intention that my visit should be brief on this occasion as Miss Bennet is still in mourning. I pray that I might be permitted to call again on another occasion."

Mrs. Gardiner was all assurances on that point and she thanked him again for calling with news of Jane.

She sat down after he was gone and looked at Elizabeth. "He seemed a most polite and affable gentleman. As he did when we met at Pemberley." She took up her needlework. "A true gentleman, who is not too proud to visit a Cheapside address."

Elizabeth took up her own sewing. "No person who had met you could possibly think they were too superior to you."

Mrs. Gardiner smiled at her sewing. "Thank you, dear. But you know that is not true. However, Mr. Darcy seems very amiable, and I hope he does call again."

CHAPTER 5

*M*r. Darcy did call again. In fact, he became quite expected, about twice a week. He would bow to the ladies, and ask gravely after Elizabeth's health.

Then he would sit with them for an hour over tea and cakes, which Mrs. Gardiner now made sure were provided as soon as he had arrived.

After Elizabeth had been in London around a month, she moved into half-mourning, and her uncle and aunt began to gently insist she attended some small functions with them. Inevitably, she found that Mr. Darcy was there too, and after going to two or three, she began to suspect that her aunt was in collusion with him, because she could not imagine that he would normally attend such events in circles outside those in which he normally moved.

Going home that evening with her aunt and uncle, she taxed them on the matter, and her aunt laughingly admitted to the deception.

"I am not in the slightest bit inclined to hide my part in the matter, Lizzy. I think he is an eminently suitable gentleman for you, and when he proposes to you, you must accept him. I believe you cannot do better."

She stared in amazement. "Aunt, I think you are mistaken. He will not propose to me. Oh, I agree he is being affable, but you heard from us all how proud and disagreeable he was at Meryton when we first met him, about how much he felt the company beneath him and how cold and unfeeling he was."

"I heard all that at the time, Lizzy, you remember well. But he has most certainly changed and you must allow that he has been most pleasant in his manner to us, and most diligent in his visits to you, too. I tell you, you cannot do better for yourself, and there you will be settled and happy."

She leaned forward in the rattling carriage. "I think you will hurt him most grievously were you to refuse his hand and you have no cause to do that."

Elizabeth looked reproachfully at her aunt. "I know that you married Uncle Gardiner for love, and you have made the happiest of unions. But many marriages I observe which have been made with expedience in mind, have not struck me with the same satisfaction to be observed in them. So I am resolved to marry for love."

Mrs. Gardiner smiled complacently at her husband. "I understand what you are saying, Lizzy, and I would not wish to disabuse you of your intentions. But Mr. Darcy has been most attentive. Do you not feel the manner of him, and the frequency with which he visits, are indicative of his feelings towards you?"

Elizabeth felt her cheeks blushing hot and looked away.

"And do you begin to feel anything for him in return, Lizzy?" her aunt enquired laughingly.

Elizabeth began to wish she had not made the opening remark in this sally, but fortunately her uncle intervened on her behalf.

"You ladies need to leave this subject for the rest of the evening and continue in the morning, when I am safely gone to work."

"Yes, Uncle Gardiner," Elizabeth agreed meekly, and the moment passed.

Twice more in the following week, Mr. Darcy called at the house, sat gravely and drank his tea.

Conversation was made, and, after a few moments, Mrs. Gardiner made her excuses about checking on the children with their governess and left them briefly alone.

Once alone, he appeared more agitated, and Elizabeth was obliged to venture a small comment on how lively the two little boys were, unlike their elder sisters and how much energy they had.

Mr. Darcy seized on the topic with relief, and stated that he was in the way of thinking that a country life for active young children was better for the child and very much easier on the nerves of their parents, for the children could spend much time outdoors.

"You are correct, sir." Elizabeth continued her sewing. "Most small children, unless they are sickly, benefit very much from many hours spent running around outside in the fresh air." She recollected her childhood. "My own family was just the same, and I developed my love of the countryside from my father." She stopped to remember him sorrowfully. "He loved the outdoors when I was a young child."

Mr. Darcy leaned forward. "You still miss him very much," he observed quietly.

Elizabeth dabbed at her face with her handkerchief. "I am sorry, Mr. Darcy. I need to stop thinking about times past."

He shook his head. "I beg to disagree. Thinking of your father is very painful now. But if you maintain the practice, in time you will come to remember him with a love and contentment of the time that you had together." He looked inwards.

"I loved my mother very much, and my pain was much extended when I did not allow myself to think of her for many months after her death."

Elizabeth looked at him, it was the first time he had told her something so personal from his own life. "Thank you, Mr. Darcy. It must be hard to talk about her to a stranger."

He smiled at that. "Do you still feel we are strangers to each other, Miss Bennet? I would hope that we are becoming friends, or maybe you would allow us to be acquaintances, if you feel friends is currently too strong a word?"

Elizabeth continued dabbing at her face to hide the fact that she needed to take a very large, shaky breath. Goodness! He might soon be going to propose marriage as her aunt had surmised.

"I like the word friends," she said very softly.

"I am glad you do," he said very solemnly, and shortly afterwards he took his leave.

THREE DAYS later Mr. Darcy called again, but this time he did not sit down when invited to do so.

"It is a very pleasant day, Miss Bennet. I wonder if it might be enjoyable for you to walk with me a short way down the street? There is a small park at the end, where we may stroll before returning back here."

Elizabeth looked at her aunt, unsure whether this was allowed at the current point in her mourning.

"What a splendid idea!" Aunt Gardiner clearly approved. "Hurry and get your hat, Lizzy. I will entertain Mr. Darcy while he waits for you."

Elizabeth hastily dropped her sewing and hurried up to her room. She quickly tidied herself and fitted the bonnet on her head, brushing the black crepe down with her hand in lieu of time to do it properly.

Then she hastened downstairs, her heart lighter than it had been for many weeks.

CHAPTER 6

*H*e was standing waiting for her in the hall, with Mrs. Gardiner standing by approvingly.

"Not too long, now, Mr. Darcy. She has not been out for some time."

He watched Elizabeth as she slowed down the final few stairs. There was warm regard in his eyes, so different from the first time he'd looked at her and told Mr. Bingley *"... she is tolerable; but not handsome enough to tempt me."*

She pushed that thought away, liking the way he looked at her now very much better than remembering that first time.

He turned to Mrs. Gardiner. "Do not concern yourself, madam. I will take the greatest of care with Miss Bennet's health and we will be back before you know it."

She simply beamed upon him, and waved them off in great good humour. Elizabeth knew that she would be all curiosity to know the subject of their conversation later that day.

They turned down towards the City, and strolled slowly along the great, bustling street. Elizabeth put up her parasol to keep the sun off her face and walked along beside Mr. Darcy, who seemed quietly content.

She felt a lively interest in the world around her and wondered that she had not walked out before now. She missed her father, of course she did, but hiding away in the house would not bring him back. She began composing a letter to him in her mind, imagining how he would respond. He would, of course, ask how soon she would be coming home - *for I miss you, Lizzy. There is no good conversation without you here.*

She sighed.

"I am sorry, Miss Bennet. Does the sight of the busy street distress you? Should we return to the house?"

"No, I am not distressed, Mr. Darcy. I am, of course, thinking of my father, but it is a more gentle melancholy now." She looked up at his face.

"I am very much enjoying the chance to walk out. Thank you for accompanying me."

"It is an honour, Miss Bennet. I'm very happy you are enjoying it." He looked around. "I have not often had the opportunity to explore this part of London. It has its own fascination."

"It certainly does." Elizabeth watched the ladies walking by, looking into shop windows, sitting in the coffee shops and proceeding with their lives. Hers had screeched to a halt two months ago, and she could only now begin to imagine moving on.

They came to a small park area, with carefully placed trees lining a gravel path through the lawns. As they strolled along, Mr. Darcy enquired as to when she had last heard from her sister.

She smiled at the thought of Jane. "She is a diligent correspondent, sir. She seems to be very happy at Netherfield, although there is still some melancholy in the letters. It was such an abrupt change to all our lives, and I understand that Mama is being difficult on many occasions."

He nodded understandingly. "Mr. Bingley is delighted with her company. She and Miss Bingley are most friendly and they are beginning to go out occasionally now that the mourning period is coming towards its end."

"Indeed," Elizabeth murmured. "I am happy

on her behalf that she has stayed there, although I miss her company here very much. We often stayed in town together."

"I have heard that," he said gravely.

After another turn around the little park, he began to speak. "Forgive me if I am talking out of turn, but I was thinking of going to Netherfield to dinner one night next week. Perhaps we could prevail upon your aunt to chaperone you and then you could both travel in my coach. We would stay the night, and maybe the following morning. It would give you time to talk to your sister and perhaps a brief visit to your mother and younger sisters, which you could curtail by reference to the return journey."

Elizabeth stopped walking and stared up at him. "Do you mean I could go and see Jane next week? Would that really be possible? Oh, you have the most wonderful ideas, Mr. Darcy." She began walking, much faster than before. "Let us go back to the house now and see if Aunt Gardiner can be persuaded."

He laughed. "I take it that you are in favour of the idea, Miss Bennet."

"Indeed. I think it is an idea that cannot wait now you have put it into my head. I must speak to Aunt Gardiner at once."

She walked quite fast back towards the house

at the quieter end of the street, thinking of nothing but the delightful thought of being able to embrace her sister and have a long, relaxed conversation with her.

She hurried up the steps, sensing Mr. Darcy's amusement.

"Aunt! Aunt Gardiner! You will never guess what we might do next week!" She knew she wasn't being very ladylike, but for the first time for ages she was happy and felt some joy in life.

"What is it, Lizzy? What has happened?" Her aunt appeared in the doorway from the drawing room. "Come on in and tell me what you are so excited about." She smiled at Elizabeth, looking happy at her niece's enthusiasm.

"And you, Mr. Darcy. I have had the tea made and some new pastries purchased for us today."

He bowed gallantly. "You always have something different to offer, madam. I thank you."

Elizabeth began telling her aunt all about the proposed trip before she had even removed her bonnet, and sat down with eager excitement, to see what she thought of it.

"I am pleased to see you looking so well, Lizzy. You have a wonderful colour in your cheeks and I can see how much this trip will mean to you." Mrs. Gardiner turned to Mr. Darcy.

"What a kind suggestion. Just the right thing for Elizabeth to have to look forward to."

He looked a little embarrassed at such effusive thanks. "It is nothing. I wish to visit Netherfield briefly, as business is keeping me in London longer than I had planned."

"It is such wonderful news. May I communicate it to Jane in my next letter to her, Mr. Darcy? Or would you prefer to make the arrangements first with Mr. Bingley?" Elizabeth was trying very hard to keep calm and ladylike.

He smiled at her excitement. "By all means tell her when you write. I am sure because of the tone of your communication she will know that there is something amiss otherwise. But you will need to wait on the exact date until I can make the arrangements with my business as to which day is most expeditious."

Elizabeth nodded. "Of course. I will do that." She knew her eyes were shining with pleasure. "Thank you so much for the offer, and also for taking me out for a walk. I had forgotten how much pleasure I get from walking. Even in town there is so much to see."

Half an hour later, he took his leave, bowing at each of the ladies, and protesting that he would inform them as soon as he knew which day they would make their journey.

Elizabeth sat close to her aunt as the children tumbled around them that evening.

"I think he is going to propose to you very soon, Lizzy. He is being most attentive and going to such trouble to please you. Do you not agree?"

Elizabeth smiled into the flames of the fire behind the iron fire guard. "I think you might be right, Aunt." She thought joyfully of the events of the day. She knew that feeling of happy anticipation inside her when she heard him at the door. She knew contentment when they conversed and she enjoyed the repartee, and was pleased when he chuckled at some humorous comment she made.

"And what do you think your answer will be when he does ask you?" Mrs. Gardiner was keenly interested in her niece's life, and although she would see much less of her once she was married, the fact that Pemberley was in Derbyshire made up for its distance in her eyes. Lambton in Derbyshire was the place Mrs. Gardiner would most like to live, had her husband's business not demanded the family lived in London.

Elizabeth felt her face grow hot and knew she was going very pink with embarrassment.

"You are going to accept him, aren't you?"

Her aunt was determined to get her answer. "He quite clearly loves you and wishes to look after you in every way possible."

"Yes." Elizabeth needed to say no more, for her aunt rose and embraced her.

"Oh, this will be so exciting! There will be much to plan and we will have to see whether London or Meryton will be the most convenient place." She was struck by a sudden thought. "Perhaps he will wait until Mr. Bingley is accepted by Jane and you will have a joint wedding from Netherfield." She continued happily making plans for a dozen different scenarios, none of which was compatible with another, until Elizabeth's head ached with all the possibilities.

CHAPTER 7

*T*he next morning, she was feeling much better, and over breakfast she decided that she would walk down Cheapside again and this time, take a look in the shops, for she had seen some interesting places yesterday, but had not then wished to prevail upon Mr. Darcy to stop.

"Elizabeth, I must suggest that you should not go alone." Mrs. Gardiner was dubious about her proposal. "It is not seemly if you are to become a great lady. I know that people of our status do, and you are used to living a free life at Longbourn. However, your behaviour will be expected to be very different if you are to accept Mr. Darcy."

"Oh, Aunt!" Elizabeth looked reproachful. "I need to be free right up until I cannot. And in truth, I think that Mr. Darcy loves me for who I am, not some imaginary great lady. I will walk just along the road to the little park, and then I will return home at once."

"But what if Mr. Darcy calls? You know it is usually in the mornings."

"But, Aunt, he was here yesterday. He will not yet have an answer for the date we are to travel to Netherfield. So I would not expect him until tomorrow at the very soonest."

Her aunt had to acknowledge the truth of that, and she sighed. "Well, Lizzy, if you must, I suppose you will come to no great harm."

"Dear Aunt Gardiner, you care so much for me. Thank you so very much for taking me in. I do not know what would have happened had you not taken over after Papa died and helped us get Mama settled and everything so well organised."

Mrs. Gardiner lifted her face for the affectionate kiss her niece gave her, and Elizabeth took the stairs two at a time, enjoying her new feeling of energy and happiness.

Choosing her favourite hat even though it didn't have the mourning crepe on it, she thought for a moment. No, her father would not have minded. *Be happy, Lizzy*, he'd have said. *Be happy*.

She hastened down the stairs.

"I will be back within the half-hour, Aunt!" she

called as she went to the door. There was no reply, and Elizabeth realised that her aunt had probably gone to pay her usual visit to the schoolroom to see what the governess was teaching the children today.

The housekeeper let her out of the door with a smile, and she stood on the step and took a deep breath.

She missed her father, of course she did. It had all been such a terrible shock and everything had happened in such a rush, when they had to get out of Longbourn so fast.

But life had moved on. Being with the Gardiners here in London had helped her to see that life could still be secure and happy. And that Mr. Darcy had opened his establishment here and called on her regularly, showing understanding for her loss, but still showing her that her life was not hopeless, that was a great help to her, too.

She stepped down to the pathway and began to stroll slowly along in the sunshine. The paths were crowded, and the road was thronged with coaches and carts, busy and noisy.

She was certain that she would see Mr. Darcy again tomorrow. Then next week, she would be travelling with him to Netherfield, dining there and seeing Jane again. She would see a lot of Mr. Darcy over those two days. A feeling of excitement and happiness suffused her. She was quite decided that he would propose to her very soon, perhaps at Netherfield.

And from her sister's correspondence, she also gained the impression that matrimonial joy might not be far off for her too.

She smiled happily into the nearest shop window. Perhaps even as early as next week, there would be some happy news to share with family and friends.

She pulled her thoughts back into the present, and looked more closely at the hats in the milliner's shop. Lydia and Kitty would be in transports of delight at the variety and quality, so much more than the simple choices in Meryton.

She smiled in recollection and looked around. The milliner's shop in Meryton had but one advantage over this one — at Meryton had been the opportunity to meet and speak with dashing young officers in their regimentals.

Then she shook her head, wondering how long it would take Lydia to grow up and be less flighty. She sighed, hoping that she would be happy in that unfortunate marriage, but not really believing it possible.

She moved on down the road, enjoying the freedom of being able to stop and gaze or move on. She had never done it before. Always Kitty or

Lydia would be hurrying her on, or dragging her backwards. And she had rarely been interested in shopping alone.

She found herself at the bottom of the road, with her senses almost reeling at the profusion of colours and sounds she'd experienced.

She saw a shop window which appeared to have masses of flowers on display, something she'd never seen before and she stepped forward. She would only look at that, just around the corner and then she would go back to the house as she had promised.

The flowers were amazing. Elizabeth had never seen such a variety and some of the lilies were completely new to her except from paintings in books. They must have come from some glasshouses to be bought by servants from the very top establishments. They would make eye-catching arrangements.

She made a mental note to bring Jane here at the next opportunity she had.

A few sharp cries and distant shouts attracted her attention, and she looked around to see what was happening.

A heavy coach was careering down the road, swaying dangerously. The four horses were plunging and kicking, and the few men who tried to grab at the reins and harnesses were soon thrown off and some of them were thrown to the ground.

Elizabeth stared in shock, stepping back to the shelter of the building. She saw one small group of shoppers scattered by the runaways, and two women vanished under the wheels, a high, thin scream cut short.

Ladies on the path were screaming now and the horses appeared to be even more frightened. The coach neared where Elizabeth was standing and she glanced around. There was nowhere to go, but she thought it would miss her as it veered off towards the middle of the road.

But, almost in slow motion, it tipped over as it turned too sharply and Elizabeth, frozen, saw it looming over her. But she was in slow motion too. There was nowhere to go, no time to move. She barely got her arm up in front of her face, when the whole thing fell onto her, throwing her onto the ground. She had a moment of terror, before the stunning blow as her head hit the path.

Then there was nothing.

CHAPTER 8

*P*ain. A deep, throbbing headache. She tried to lift her hand to her face to hide her eyes where the brightness hurt, even through her closed lids. But then her arm hurt too and she gave up trying to move. A low moan escaped her lips.

"Don't try and move, Miss Soames. I am a doctor. You have had a nasty blow on the head, but you are being well cared for by your father. Everything is going to be perfectly all right."

"Who …?"

"No, don't try and talk. We will do everything that is needed. You have been brought home and will need to stay in bed for the time being. Your maid has brought you some broth. You must have just a little."

She opened her eyes. A man was putting on his coat and talking in a low voice to an older man who was seeing him to the door. She looked around. She was in a bedroom where the heavy curtains were drawn to keep out the light. A maid, looking frightened, was sitting beside the bed, a bowl of gruel in her hands.

She frowned and winced as a sharp pain went through her head. The older man hurried back to the bedside.

"Don't distress yourself, Sarah. You will be quite all right. The doctor himself has said so."

She looked at him. She knew she had never seen him before in her life. And who was Sarah?

"Who — who are you?"

He looked sorrowful. "I'm your Papa, Sarah. You know me. You've been taking such good care of me since your Mama died, and now it's my turn to take really good care of you until you're well again."

"But I'm not Sarah."

He smiled kindly. "Of course you are. We had been to the gallery and were returning here when the horses were spooked by something or other. The coach overturned and I could not stop you getting a most severe bang on your head." He looked anxious. "Please forgive me, my dear, I would not for anything have allowed you to receive such an injury if it had been in my power."

Something was very wrong. "I am not Sarah."

But who was she? No name came into her head, no instant knowledge of who she was. Panic beat at the edges of her mind. "Who — where am I?"

"Sarah, my dear. Please be calm," the man entreated her. She began to shake her head, but stopped as the ache threatened to worsen.

"Kate, bring a compress for Miss Soames' head." His voice became crisper, sharper and he placed his hand over hers on the bed. But it wasn't comforting, it was the cold hand of a stranger and made her feel even lonelier. She shrank back against the pillows.

He smiled at her. "You will feel better in the morning." When the maid came back into the room, he left.

The maid placed a cold wet cloth over her forehead, and she shivered. Who was she? Where was she? What had happened?

She looked at the maid. "How long have I been here?"

The girl looked very frightened. "Mr. Soames had you carried here from the accident yesterday, madam."

"Yesterday!" She wondered at that. "I'm not

supposed to be here! They'll be worried about me."

"Who will, madam?"

She wondered why the maid didn't refer to her by name. If only her head didn't ache so, she could try and work this out.

"How long have you been my maid, Kate?" She was sure she didn't have a maid.

"Not very … I mean, quite a while, Miss S… Soames."

She let the maid feed her a little broth. Something was very wrong, but she couldn't work out what it was. A strange weakness was stealing over her and she felt sleep wiping her thoughts away.

IT WAS SEVERAL DAYS LATER, and she was sitting up in an armchair by the fire in the bedroom for the first time. Her father — it seemed so wrong, thinking of him like that — had been to visit her and been encouraged that she was getting so much better.

But a deep sadness and loneliness seemed to have settled over her, and she didn't seem to be able to think of any way out of the situation in which she found herself.

A heaviness and dullness of mind seemed to

be foreign to her, but as they enveloped her, she began to accept her situation. Perhaps she was Sarah, a dull, heavy creature, who had no future or spark of life.

A ring at the doorbell downstairs roused her from her torpor. Perhaps it was the doctor again. He seemed to be the only visitor to the house. Slowly, she rose to her feet and went towards the door which was ajar. Perhaps she would hear something. She did.

A new voice, crisp and strangely compelling. "Good morning. We have a few questions, if we may enter?"

A murmur of dissent from the staff, then the steward's voice.

"What do you wish to know, constable? I may not be able to say much as Mr. Soames is not at home this morning."

"I understand. It has come to my attention that it was Mr. Soames' coach that was involved in the accident off Cheapside last week. Following on from that, we believe that he assisted a young lady who had been involved. They entered a hansom cab and returned here. Is that true?"

"Constable, that is true. Thankfully, Mr. Soames was unhurt. His daughter, Sarah, was injured, but the doctor has been attending her regularly and she is recovering."

"I have received a statement from a witness who states that the young lady concerned was not travelling in the coach, but was out walking and struck by the coach as it overturned."

Another voice broke in impatiently. "Is the young lady available to be visited?" She shivered, did she recognise that voice?

"Sir, she has not yet been well enough to come downstairs. I have told you all I can, I will tell Mr. Soames you have called and I suggest that you attend tomorrow when he will be able to give you the assurances you need."

The voice again, the one that sent a shiver of recognition down her. "We will return tomorrow, and I will bring a lady with me who might be able to visit the young lady in her rooms, with the consent of Mr. Soames."

"I will inform Mr. Soames. Sir, Constable." The steward's obsequious tones told her that he was bowing the visitors out.

Then she heard him calling the staff and she listened carefully. He called them and instructed them to start packing up as it was certain that Mr. Soames would wish to leave this establishment today.

She retreated back to her chair. What did all this mean? Who had that voice belonged to? The maid arrived with a tray of tea and small cakes. She decided to ask her what was going on.

"Who were those men, Kate? It is unusual to have visitors here apart from the doctor."

"Yes, madam. It had not been unusual, only since you have been ill, as Mr. Soames did not wish you to be disturbed unnecessarily."

"Did the visitor leave a calling card?"

"I do not know." The maid seemed frightened and hurried out of the room. Was it to prevent being asked more questions?

She sipped her tea. She couldn't face the cakes, still often feeling very nauseous. The doctor had said that was a result of her injury and it would get better slowly. She wondered if her lassitude and feeling of dullness, of feeling unable to make any decisions of her own, whether that would pass. Or had she always been like this? That thought frightened her more than anything.

CHAPTER 9

Mr. Soames came home, and within a very short time came hurrying into her room.

"Sarah, my dear, I have decided to leave London. I have had a conference with your physician and he feels that you will benefit very much from clean country air and the quieter living."

He hastened toward the door. "I have engaged a coach and four, so please hurry on with your coat and hat."

The maid hurried in as he left the room and helped her with her toilette.

"Are you packed yourself, Kate?" She was puzzled at the haste, and Kate went to the closet and removed her two spare dresses and a nightgown.

"No, Miss … er … Miss Soames. I remain at this establishment and I will see you next time you are in town." She laid the clothes on the bed and began folding them to pack in the small case.

As she watched the maid, she was struck with how little she had here, and that the dresses were new. She had not noticed that before. Tears came to her eyes. Who was she? And why did she not have a better sense of her past?

"Do not distress yourself, madam. Mr. Soames has a lovely little estate in Dorset. It is very pretty and looks out over the sea."

"Dorset?" Surely if she was his daughter, she would know that?

"Sarah! Sarah, are you ready yet?" Her father hurried into her room. "Oh, good, you are ready." He looked at the maid.

"Take Miss Soames' bag down to Mr. Fuller, please. He is supervising the loading of the coach." He gave a slight grimace as though he was in pain.

"Are you all right, sir?" She was concerned for him.

"I am well, my dear. And remember, you must call me Papa, not *sir*. You have always called me Papa."

"Papa," she said obediently, and he beamed at her.

"Let's go downstairs, my dear Sarah. We can walk very slowly."

She was rather dizzy as they descended the stairs, it seemed a very long time since she'd walked more than a few paces, and he kept her in the hall for a few moments, until his steward signalled him.

Then he led her through the front door, down the steps and helped her into the hired coach. He leaned over and drew the blind down over the window.

"I don't want the sun to seem too bright for you, my dear."

"Thank you — Papa."

The steward shut the door and Mr. Soames drew down the blind there too. They felt the coach rock as someone climbed up outside and then it jolted and they moved off.

He didn't speak to her much, just patted her arm and sat there, tense.

"What concerns you, Papa?" She wondered what the matter was, he had seemed distracted since she had had the accident. "Is it something I have done?"

"No, no. Not at all, Sarah. We will just be better when we are clear of the town. The doctor assures me of that."

"That is good news."

They fell silent and after a few moments, she realised he was dozing in his corner.

They drove on for what seemed like hours, and after a while, she daringly raised the blind on her side of the coach. They seemed to be out of the city now, and there were few houses. The sight of rolling fields lifted her spirits in a manner she didn't recognise and she watched the changing scenery before the motion made her feel rather sick, when she closed her eyes.

It was dusk before they drew up outside an inn, and she felt the coach rock as someone climbed down from outside. The steward, Fuller, came to the door of the coach, and Mr. Soames glanced at her.

"Stay here for just a moment, Sarah." He got out of the coach and he conversed earnestly with his steward.

Then he nodded and turned to her. "We are going to get another coach and continue on for some hours, Sarah. I confess I am anxious to get to my estate soon and I hope that you will be able to sleep on the journey. But for now, we will eat."

He assisted her down the step and into the inn where the steward had arranged a private room. She and Mr. Soames ate a hasty meal, although he didn't seem able to eat much, and she began to be concerned for him.

"How long will it take us to get to your estate, Papa?" she tried to think of some topic of conversation.

"A few days." He seemed distracted.

"Kate said how pretty it was, looking out over the sea."

He started. "No, no, she must have been mistaken. It is in the hills."

"Oh." She stopped to think about that, quite sure that she had not misheard what Kate had said.

A FEW MINUTES LATER, they were climbing up into a different coach. The steward assisted her up the step, as Mr. Soames seemed to be walking very slowly.

She sat quiet on the seat. Something was very wrong. But her head ached, and she was so tired. The coach wasn't going fast, the carriage lights didn't allow for that, so she wondered why it was necessary not to stop at an inn for the night.

THEY DID STOP the next night, the countryside hilly and wild. Mr. Soames seemed more cheerful then, and more willing to stop at mealtimes. But he seemed greyer, thinner and his appetite was very poor.

She found herself beginning to worry about him, to be trying to cheer him up and she started asking questions about her younger life. He told stories of the family when she was a child, anecdotes that seemed true, which confused her even more.

She was heartily sick of days of driving, changing coaches when the horses were tired, and endless different bedrooms in inns of varying quality.

"Papa, when are we going to get there? I didn't think Dorset was so far away."

"Dorset? Who said anything about Dorset? We are approaching Newcastle in Northumberland. So we are nearly there, Sarah."

That evening, she saw him conversing with the steward and handing him a letter. Then he came back to the inn and sat with her over their dinner.

The following morning, she climbed into yet another coach for the endless journey. She was worried about her travelling companion.

"Papa, I feel that if we do not get there soon, we ought to stop for several days. It will give you a chance to rest and regain your strength. You look so tired."

"Thank you, my dear. You will be pleased to know that we are very close now. Mr. Fuller went ahead last night with instructions to open up the house and we will be there later today."

"Oh, that is wonderful news, Papa! Tell me about the house and the garden, please. I still cannot recall it."

He smiled. "It will be a pleasant surprise for you, I hope."

She leaned over and watched out of the window. She hoped it would not be long until she was there, wherever there was.

CHAPTER 10

*M*r. Darcy took the steps two at a time and rang the doorbell. He knew his news would not be welcome and he was so tired. The housekeeper opened the door to him and he nodded to her.

"Come in, Mr. Darcy, sir." The woman curtsied. "I will tell the master and mistress that you are here."

He waited impatiently, shifting from one foot to the other. Mrs. Gardiner hurried from the drawing room, followed more slowly by her husband.

"Oh, Mr. Darcy! Do you have news for us?" But she didn't need to hear his answer. She must have seen it in his face, because her own expression showed open disappointment.

"I'm sorry, I am not being hospitable. Come in and I will order tea."

He followed her silently into the great room, seeming so empty now that Elizabeth was no longer there. His hostess indicated his usual chair and he sat down, sighing deeply.

"So, they did not go to Dorset?" she asked.

He shook his head. "No. I was so sure they would go there, the steward was the only servant they took, so I convinced myself he would immediately go somewhere familiar. As you know I rode the overnight express to get there, so I must have reached there before them."

He stared at the fireplace. "They have received no instructions to open up, and I waited three days, calling at all the inns on the main London roads. There has been no sign of them."

He stood up and began to pace around. "I have instructed the local magistrate and there is attention on the matter. Should they appear, nothing will be done to arouse any suspicion, but I will be notified at once." He turned to Mr. Gardiner. "I have given them this address, and if anything comes, you are to read it at once, and send word to me, wherever I am."

Mr. Gardiner nodded acquiescence without speaking.

Darcy walked to the window, and looked out

at the street. "He did have a daughter named Sarah. I visited the local parson. The family was much loved in the locality. Mr. Soames has a reputation for being a kind and just man. But his wife died last year, of a consumptive disease, and he was overcome with grief. Within a week, Sarah caught a fever and died also. He was distraught and utterly alone." His voice was clipped and brusque. "I visited the graves. She was one year younger than Elizabeth."

He turned and saw Mrs. Gardiner's eyes were filled with tears.

"That poor man."

Darcy's lips tightened. "Yes. He left Dorset within days of Sarah's funeral and opened up his London house to grieve away from all the memories, I would suppose." His voice hardened. "But that is no reason to abduct another young lady lying injured on the street. Moreover, a young lady who appears not to remember who she is." He crossed the room again, unable to keep still.

"I went to the house and spoke very forcefully to the staff. They are all of the settled opinion that he had taken her to Dorset. They have no idea where else they might have gone. The young maid who was tasked with being her personal servant says that Elizabeth has no idea who she is. She has accepted Mr. Soames' story and the staff were all instructed to go along with the fabrication. They are very loyal to their master."

He dropped into the chair. "I blame myself. I blame myself utterly. If I had only asked you to accompany me to the house that day when I went there, I am convinced the constable might have insisted you see her. Then we could have brought her back here to be nursed back to health."

"You must not blame yourself, Mr. Darcy." Mrs. Gardiner repeated the assurances she had often given before he dashed off to Dorset. "You were in a hurry to find her and the constable would not wait for you to find me."

He nodded. "But I am going to find her. If I have to search every inch of England I will find her."

"Of course you will. Elizabeth needs you to help her in the future and keep her safe."

He rose again. "Yes. Thank you for your confidence." His eyes fell on the small portrait on the mantel. "That small watercolour of her by Miss Jane Bennet is a very good likeness. May I borrow it and get a copy painted? I will then return it to you before I take the copy with me to ask coach drivers and innkeepers if they have seen her."

"Of course. That is an excellent idea." Mrs. Gardiner rose and picked up the small picture.

She ran her finger affectionately over the image before handing it to Mr. Darcy.

He took it and stood, hesitant, for a moment. "Have you heard how Miss Jane Bennet has been since she received the news? I have not yet been home to see if there is news from Netherfield."

Mrs. Gardiner looked sad. "She is extremely distressed, as you can imagine. She wanted to come immediately to London, thinking that you would be bringing her here when you found her in Dorset. But of course, that has not happened, so it is as well that she stays safe at Netherfield for the time being."

He nodded. "Please assure her that I will write to her immediately when I have any news whatsoever, and arrange that they might be together as soon as is possible." He hesitated. "Of course, if Elizabeth recovers her memory, she might well write to Jane first, or yourself, depending on what she remembers." He thought for a moment. "Perhaps you might impress upon Miss Bennet the need to let us know so that Mr. Soames is not warned before I can get there to prevent her being hidden away again."

"I will write to her in that vein this very evening, Mr. Darcy." Mrs. Gardiner looked at him. "I know you will find her, please do not rebuke yourself, and you must join us for dinner.

You look as if you have not eaten well for many days."

He smiled slightly. "You are most kind, madam. Please do not be offended if I decline your generous offer this evening. I will return home and go to bed very early. I intend to be up with the sunrise and I will get this portrait copied and be around the hire cabs before they get much work."

He bowed. "With your consent, I will return tomorrow evening and inform you of what I have found out."

CHAPTER 11

*S*he stood on top of the small hill and looked around. It was a quiet day, the first that the wind had not been almost too strong for her. She drew in great lungfuls of air and decided that she really quite liked Northumberland.

If only Papa were not so ill, she might be able to get out and about more often. She was sure that if she could do that, somehow the fogginess in her mind and the bad dreams would begin to fade. But Papa was so unwell, she did not often like to leave him.

"Sarah," he would call, and she would go hastening into his room and fetch him another blanket, or read to him, whatever he wanted.

They had been at Blantyre House for nearly a

month now, and she was beginning to settle down and feel more at home. She had tried to put behind her the suspicions that this house was as new to him as it was to her. The staff had definitely all been new, she watched as they learned their way around the house and the routine that Mr. Soames demanded.

However, as this month was passing, she was consumed with worry for her Papa. She spoke to his steward, and they agreed he needed to see the doctor. The doctor had called and recommended he see a specialist physician in Newcastle and spoken of special foods.

So, the next day, she was going with Papa to Newcastle. The appointment had been made and Fuller, who had obviously been with his master for many years, was adding extra cushions and blankets to the coach to make the journey as comfortable as possible.

The steward had become friendlier to her as she showed her care for Papa, and he accepted her presence more readily. However, she was uncomfortable in his presence and didn't like the way he sometimes looked at her.

At first he had been suspicious when she wanted to walk outside the grounds, he'd followed her at a distance and asked her where she wanted to go.

But now, he seemed to have acknowledged that she only walked in the hills and was not looking to see anyone. There was no one to see, anyway. They were many miles from the nearest houses, and she wondered why Papa had chosen this place to stay.

She turned for home, not wanting to be away too long. But first, she stopped and scanned the landscape. In her dreams she would see a tall, dark man, a man with a proud bearing, and dark, burning eyes. He would be standing there, watching for her. She thought he was a stranger, but he couldn't be a stranger if she was dreaming about him, could he? But, as always, there was no one to be seen and, dejected, she made her way home.

The next day, they drove to Newcastle and she watched Papa carefully. In one month, he was a completely different man. Eaten up with disease, she knew deep inside that he had not long to live.

Outside the doctor's practice, she and the steward helped him down from the coach and she took him inside. The doctor was attentive and thorough. She watched him as he examined Papa and saw him shake his head.

So she was prepared when he sat down and spoke to them. He talked of an obstruction and how important it was to try and keep Papa's strength up by preparing food that was easy to swallow, to drink plenty of water and soup, and recommending the taking of laudanum from the physician at home if pain prevented him from eating.

She didn't feel that anything much was going to help Papa, and she knew he knew it too, although he would not speak of it to her.

She helped him from the house, towards the coach where the steward was waiting. But as he moved forward to assist her, there was a loud, strident voice.

"Lizzy! Lizzy! How exciting to see you here!" A young woman ran up to her, shouting excitedly and dragging a gentleman behind her.

She shrank back against Papa, and he staggered a little. She grasped his arm, supporting him as he supported her too.

"Who …?"

The gentleman bowed. "It is a wonderful surprise, Miss Bennet, to see you here. We did not know you were in this city."

She stared wildly at him. Who were they? How did they know her?

"Who are you?" she looked at the young woman who laughed gaily.

"Oh, what a joke, Lizzy. Pretending you do not know me!" the young woman elbowed her sharply. "Wickham, don't you think it so amusing a joke?"

"I am not pretending. I do not know you." She could feel her heart beating wildly. Was she about to find out who she was?

The steward stepped forward. "Miss Soames, we must help your father into the coach. He is fatigued."

"Oh, yes, of course. Please excuse me." She turned to Papa, who had gone quite a grey colour, and took a step with him towards the coach.

"Now, Lizzy." The young woman sounded quite reproachful. "Of course you know your own sister! I know you are jealous that I got married first even though I am the youngest. But it is no good pretending to me that you aren't Lizzy Bennet. I knew you straight away!"

"Sarah, I need you." Papa's voice was raspy and gasping.

"Yes, Papa." She turned to the young couple.

"I am sorry. My name is Miss Sarah Soames. You are mistaking me for someone else. Good-bye." Her concern for Papa quite overrode her manners and she climbed into the coach after him and nodded at the steward, who leapt aboard and urged the coachman to drive on.

She leaned over to Papa, and adjusted the cushion behind his head. "Do not let them disturb you, Papa. They must have mistaken me for some-body else. I did not recognise them at all. Neither did I like them."

He smiled weakly. "You are good to me, Sarah. Your mother would have been proud of you."

She smiled back. "Thank you, Papa. Now rest. We will be home soon."

CHAPTER 12

*M*r. Darcy stretched out as much as he could, which wasn't much in the small, low-ceilinged room. This inn was far less comfortable than those he tried to use where possible. But he needed to stay searching, and in the morning he would resume his quest.

For weeks now, he had been on the move, restless and unable to settle to anything. He had spent days searching for the coach that had taken Elizabeth and her kidnapper from that house, and had at last found the inn where they had changed coach and horses. But they had not stayed the night, instead they had driven off recklessly into the darkness.

It had taken more days and a lot of money to find out the name of the cab driver who had driven them. But it had been worth it. The coach had driven southwest for ten miles and then, in the early hours of the morning, had turned to the north.

It was the breakthrough Mr. Darcy had been looking for. Urgently, he had spent money, taken the post coaches, stopped at inn after inn. He had followed the turnpikes to the north, the northwest, the east, and drawn blank. Every night he wrote back to the Gardiners, saying where he'd been searching and giving them an address of the post in the town he planned to be at three days hence.

Each time he arrived there, a letter from Mrs. Gardiner would carry nothing but well-wishes, concern for his search. But never news of Elizabeth, news that would give him a clue where he might find her.

Despondently, he threw off his coat, and slumped in the chair. He didn't want dinner tonight, what he longed for was a little luxury, and a hot bath.

He sighed and pulled out a sheet of notepaper and a pen.

> *Dear Mrs. Gardiner,*
> *Thank you for your letter of Tuesday last,*
> *which awaited me here. I am most*
> *grateful for your constant updates of*

*news. I confess I am disappointed
that there is no positive news, but it is
better to know than not.*

*I am close to Pemberley and I propose to
be there from tomorrow for two days
to rest and think on my best course of
action. I have searched Lancashire
with no intimation that they might be
there, and will go to Pemberley
through the northern part of
Yorkshire, although I will need to
return there as it is a large county,
with many remote houses.*

*I will correspond again tomorrow as
usual.*

*My best wishes to you and to Mr.
Gardiner also.*

He threw down the pen. He hadn't decided to go to Pemberley before he wrote that, but having made that decision, he now felt it to be a good one. Georgiana deserved a little of his attention too, although his worry and concern for Elizabeth consumed all his waking thoughts, and she filled his dreams at night too.

Why had he observed the niceties and not proposed to her before her mourning was over? Mrs. Gardiner had let slip that she had discussed it and Elizabeth was minded to accept him, which made her loss all the more raw.

He strode about the room. He had to find her before she was lost to him forever, maybe married to someone else, having quite forgotten him. No, he dare not think like that.

It was scarce eight weeks since that dreadful day when a note from Mrs. Gardiner had arrived, saying that Elizabeth had not returned from her walk, and since then he hadn't slept more than a few hours before waking to think of her again.

Surely soon she might begin to recall who she really was. He had visited the top physicians in the country, discussed the course of recovery from an injury to the head, and had been much reassured that some half of victims took more than a month to recover past memories. And he had been assured that most of them did eventually recover much of what had been erased from their immediate recall.

And in that time, he had had the energy of a man possessed by his search. He was convinced that Elizabeth was now living under the name of Sarah Soames and that she was with a man who was purporting to be her father. So at least she should be safe from abuse and ruin. Soames was apparently a gentleman, and Darcy did not know whether the man really thought Elizabeth was his own Sarah, somehow come back to him, or if it was a convenient fabrication to gain her services to him.

Now all he had to do was to find them, find a man who had much to hide and did not want to be found.

Soon there would be some clue, some intimation of her or some hint that something was not quite right about a new family in a remote neighbourhood. He just had to keep searching.

LATE THE NEXT DAY, he arrived at Pemberley. Georgiana was delighted to see him, but concerned at his haggard looks.

"I declare, dear brother, that you must rest a few days before resuming your search. You will do no good if you become ill before finding her."

He acknowledged her with as much grace as he could muster, but inside, he was unable to shake off the feeling that time was becoming short, urgency was pressing. What if something happened and she ended up alone, but still not knowing who she was?

His dreams were bedevilled with concern for her and he had to force himself to sit and plan with deliberation and not rush from place to place like a moth beating out its life against a flame.

"Thank you, little sister. I am happy to see you again, but sorry it will only be for a few days. I must continue searching."

She dipped her head. "Of course you must. She must be very frightened. I hope that she can soon be here where we can give her time and space to recover."

He looked at the girl gratefully. "Thank you, Georgiana. I also hope that she will soon be here."

His manservant appeared in the doorway and bowed. His bath was ready. Darcy had never been so anxious to be finally clean. He excused himself and went upstairs.

IT WAS two days later that the letter came. Mr. Darcy was preparing for his journey to continue. So much time had passed that there was no longer any use in trying to find drivers who might have recognised her picture. He would visit every parish and listen to gossip of new arrivals. Each evening he would write to the magistrate in another parish too, to see if there was a hint that the place might warrant a visit for further searching.

But here was a letter from Mrs. Gardiner. He

smiled, she was assiduous in her correspondence.
But he had been disappointed so often that he no
longer felt a twist of excitement that today might
be the day.

Then he noticed that his name was underlined
twice on the outside of the sealed letter. It must be
something different and he tore at it in frantic
haste.

> *Dear Mr. Darcy,*
> *News at last!*
> *It is unfortunately old news, because*
> > *Lydia Wickham didn't think to send*
> > *news immediately that she had seen*
> > *Lizzy in Newcastle ...*

Darcy leapt to his feet, calling his manservant.

"James! Mr. James! Send my steward to get the
coach and he is to come with me to Newcastle.
At once."

Then he sat down to read the rest of the letter.

> *But she wrote to her mother, requesting*
> *money. In that letter, she said that it*
> *was a great joke that Elizabeth had*
> *not recognised her and Mr. Wickham*
> *the previous week in Newcastle, and*
> *why her mother had not told her that*

> *Elizabeth was living with a man she*
> *called Papa.*
> *Jane did not find out about the letter until*
> *she visited her mother two days after*
> *it had been received.*

Darcy tore at his hair in frustration and hurried back into the hall.

"Mrs. Reynolds, Mrs. Reynolds!"

And when the housekeeper appeared, he spoke hastily.

"Please call for Miss Darcy to come down here immediately. And is my coach ready?"

"I will call her at once, sir. Mr. James is packing your bag, and Mr. Reed is calling your coach away." And she bustled off.

Mr. Darcy returned to the library.

> *I am enclosing the pages of Jane's letter to*
> *me. She wrote at once, and as you can*
> *see, has copied exactly what*
> *Lydia said.*
> *I have entreated her not to write to the*
> *Wickhams, because I believe that*
> *they might alert Mr. Soames to our*
> *foreknowledge. But I cannot believe*
> *he might not go away again,*

Elizabeth having been accosted by Lydia.

He felt despair. He had to hurry.

Georgiana ran into the room. "What is the matter, Fitzwilliam? What has happened?"

Blindly, he thrust the letter at her and she skimmed it quickly. He turned and collected sheets of notepaper, pens and ink. He dare not run short of those.

"So you see I must go, and at once." He stooped to kiss his sister, who had tears in her eyes.

"Should I come with you, brother? She will need a chaperone."

He hesitated. Thought.

Then he shook his head. "Thank you for your offer, Georgiana. I may send for you very soon, and your governess will then accompany you. But it is possible they have fled again. I may need to pursue them as fast as possible while the trail is warmest."

He smiled down at her. "Be assured I will write to you soon and tell you what I know."

She curtsied. "Thank you. I will think of you and pray that your search is successfully concluded within very few days."

He looked at her with fresh eyes. She was growing into a kind and resourceful young woman. He would have to make sure she wed someone who would appreciate her strength of character.

Then he hurried from the room. He must think only of Elizabeth.

CHAPTER 13

*I*n the coach, he struggled to write legibly, asking Miss Jane Bennet to find out the address of Mr. and Mrs. Wickham and send it to him at the post house in Newcastle as soon as possible, and also asking her to convey the same information to Mrs. Gardiner.

They reached the city of Derby in time to transfer to the express coach to Newcastle, and Darcy had his steward send his own coach back to Pemberley. He and Reed then sat up overnight, trying to sleep as the swaying mail coach rattled through the darkness.

"Have you found out how long we'll take to get there, Mr. Reed?" Mr. Darcy didn't bother opening his eyes. It was too dark to see anything, anyway.

"Yes, sir. It will be late tomorrow, if you decide not to stop. Or if you wish to stop when they change horses, then not until Friday. It is one hundred and sixty miles."

"We do not stop."

"Yes, sir."

Darcy sat there, mulling over what would happen when he arrived. He would take rooms at the inn and go and get the Wickham's address which would be waiting for him in a letter from Miss Bennet. Then he must plan carefully.

He detested the thought of confronting Mr. Wickham. But it must be done, and he was prepared with a bribe if necessary. That might be the only way to ensure that the youngest sister did not blunder foolishly around and destroy his chance of finding Elizabeth. Wickham was not stupid, and he would make sure his wife did as she was told.

Yes, he would tell Wickham that any payment would only follow if Elizabeth was still there. He slid down the seat a little and began to doze. He might need a day to rest after this journey, to ensure he was thinking quickly enough to meet them.

~

HE FOUND that they didn't live in Newcastle itself. He took time to check the area and engage a coach and man for the duration, before he drove out to the northeast, towards the village of Longbenton.

Uncharacteristically hesitant, he called first to see the colonel of the regular corps where Wickham was a junior officer.

"So, how can I help you, Mr. Darcy?" the colonel waved at the manservant, who withdrew after pouring them drinks.

Darcy relaxed back in the comfortable chair, liking the man immediately. "I wish to speak to Mr. George Wickham, and I may need to ask him to come to Newcastle with me briefly to identify a location his wife referred to in a letter to her mother. I am afraid I cannot yet divulge why, although I undertake to inform you as soon as I am at liberty to do so."

The colonel made a face and took a swig of his drink. "I appreciate your candour and I am sure you will also not divulge my feelings. But you can take him away as long as you like — as long as he pays his gambling debts. If he is not careful, he will be court-martialled. And his wife is equally complicit." He glanced over at Darcy.

"Are they related in any way to you?"

"No, sir, they are not."

"Then you are a fortunate man, sir." The colonel heaved himself to his feet and rang his bell. "I will send my subaltern to show you his residence."

Darcy shook his hand. "I am indebted to you, sir. Thank you."

Within ten minutes he was striding through the barracks with the young subaltern, his coach following at a discreet distance. He wasn't ready, he did not know what to say, and he so disliked the thought of seeing Wickham again he could not think further than that.

"Mr. Wickham may not wish to speak to me," he said abruptly to the young officer. "You must say we have been sent from your colonel."

"Yes, sir." There was a quiver in the young man's voice and Darcy wondered whether the colonel was quite as affable as he had seemed.

He put his hand in his pocket and felt the folded leather cover. Nestled in there was his copy of the painting of Elizabeth. He looked at her often and just touching the case gave him the strength to do what he had to.

He waited at the side of the door to the mean little accommodation while the subaltern knocked at the door.

It opened to a housekeeper. The young officer asked, rather nervously, if Mr. and Mrs. Wickham were at home. Then he said that the colonel had sent him with a visitor for the couple, and Mr. Darcy moved into view and handed her his card.

Young Lydia Wickham appeared, loud and enthusiastic. She dismissed the subaltern with a wave, and invited Mr. Darcy in, telling her house-keeper to bring tea in a manner which raised Darcy's hackles on the servant's behalf. Then Wickham was there, his face guarded.

He bowed slightly. "To what do we owe this honour, Mr. Darcy?" He wasn't very good at hiding his emotions, but the fact that Darcy was come from the colonel was obviously playing on his mind.

Mr. Darcy wasted no time. He bowed to Lydia. "Mrs. Wickham, I understand that you saw your sister, Miss Elizabeth Bennet, in Newcastle a few weeks ago. I am here to ask you exactly where you saw her and what happened, who she was with, where she came from and where she went."

"Oh, that!" Mrs. Wickham tossed her head. "I thought it was a tremendous joke, but she hasn't been to see me and so I have given up on her! Quite given up. She always was jealous that I got married before any of them."

Mr. Darcy bit his tongue, he needed informa-tion. "I understand how you feel, Mrs. Wickham, and I am sure when she can be found, she would wish to visit you and admire your home."

He looked at Mr. Wickham. "I have the consent of your colonel that you should both come with me to Newcastle and assist me in identifying the place where you saw her."

"Well, I'm sure *I* don't want to." Lydia pouted and threw herself down on the sofa. "I have to get ready for the dance tonight at Mrs. Jones'. It will be tremendous fun."

Wickham said not a word, but Mr. Darcy knew how to make him comply. "I can of course, make sure you receive adequate compensation for your trouble." He was rewarded by a look of avarice behind the suave expression.

"Well, my dear, if the colonel wants us to go, then I suppose we need to indulge Mr. Darcy." He stepped closer.

"How much?"

Darcy stepped back. "Five hundred pounds. But half of it I will retain until Miss Bennet is located to my satisfaction. Mrs. Wickham must not discuss the matter with anyone."

Mr. Wickham turned to his wife. "Get your hat, woman. The sooner this is done, the sooner you will be home again."

"I will ready the coach." Mr. Darcy could not bear to remain in the house a moment longer, not liking that he saw the girl cringe away. But it was none of his business. She had caused his Elizabeth much grief when she ran away with that scoundrel, and she must live with her choice.

He took a deep breath as he stood on the step. He beckoned the coach, and the coachman shook the reins and moved towards the house. Reed sat watchful beside him.

Within a few moments the Wickhams came out of the house and climbed aboard the coach. Darcy followed, rapping on the roof to start them off. Thankfully the city centre was not too far.

He sat, stony-faced, while Lydia prattled on, showing off her ring, and bemoaning the loss of her father because her mother could no longer send them much extra money.

Wickham tended to ignore her, answering few of her questions. But he wouldn't meet Darcy's eyes, either, staring out of the window most of the journey.

Mr. Darcy saw no need to be too polite, until he thought maybe Elizabeth would wish to visit them once she was back. So he exerted himself to be minimally polite to her, and she became louder and more vulgar. He wondered at the family that could raise two delightful ladies such as Elizabeth and Jane, but also the deplorable, ignorant young woman in front of him.

As they drove into the centre of the city, he sat up suddenly. "So where was she when you saw her? What was she doing?"

The couple looked at each other. "Oh, Lord, I don't know," Lydia said fretfully. "You tell him, Wickham."

Mr. Wickham looked as if he much regretted being tied to her, but he was concentrated on the magical amount of five hundred pounds.

"We were walking along King Street, down towards the river. She came out of one of the large houses on the right, with a frail older man." He spoke readily, confidently.

"Can you tell me which house?" Mr. Darcy could scarcely believe he was so close.

Mr. Wickham shrugged. "Yes. It had a plate beside the door. I imagined it was the practice of a physician."

"So what happened? What was said?"

Lydia sat up. "*I* spoke to her first. I called her name, said how exciting it was to see her in the city." She frowned. "Then she asked who I was, and I told her what a joke it was that she was pretending not to know me. But I wasn't really amused, you know," she said crossly. "She does not usually play jokes like that."

He despaired at her stupidity. "So who was she with?"

She turned wounded eyes on him. "An older man, he was holding her arm. She called him Papa. Well, I know that must be part of the joke, because of course, he isn't." She frowned. "I thought she might be angry that I didn't come down to Longbourn when our father died, but he was so rude to me sometimes, calling me a silly girl, so I didn't see why I should." She turned to her husband.

"He was very rude, wasn't he?"

He patted her arm absently, looking out of the window. The coach was slowing. When it drew to a halt, Reed appeared at the window.

"King Street, Reed. The big houses on the right as you go down towards the river. The house has a plate beside the door."

"Yes, sir." Reed vanished and climbed back beside the driver.

Mr. Darcy gazed impatiently out of the window. It was still light, he had time. Maybe, maybe at last, he might be close to finding her.

"Anything else you can remember? I will make the rest of the payment when I find her, so the more you can help me, the better."

Mr. Wickham looked resentful, but he was careful not to say anything, the lure of money was too much. "She said she was not Elizabeth. I can't remember the name she used — Sarah something, I think."

"Sarah Soames." Lydia interrupted. "What a stupid name to make up! I would have thought of something much better than that."

They drew up outside a row of large imposing houses on the wide street. Mr. Darcy stepped down, letting Mr. and Mrs. Wickham follow at their own pace. He stared at the house in front of him, which had a brass plaque at the side.

"Yes, that's it." Wickham stood near him, but not too close. "That's the house she came out of. The servant had brought the coach really close, and he interrupted us when we were talking. She did as he told her to, though he was obviously only a servant."

Mr. Darcy's heart sank. His Elizabeth was intelligent and independent. He hoped she was not beaten down with illness following the accident. His urgent need to find her intensified.

"All right. Thank you. Please thank your colonel for me too, and tell him I will visit again as soon as I have news for him."

Wickham looked alarmed. "Does he know the story?"

Mr. Darcy shook his head. "No, he does not, but I have promised to tell him when I am successful." He saw no reason that Mr. Wickham should have an easy mind. He thrust money at him. "As I promised. The rest will follow if you do not frustrate my search by talking out of turn." He looked meaningfully at Mrs. Wickham, yawning and complaining, as she leaned against the coach.

"She will not talk," Wickham said shortly. "How are we to get home?"

Darcy shrugged. "You have money now for a cab. I will need the coach as soon as I have spoken to the physician."

He started up the steps, hearing an expletive from Wickham about finding a chaise to take them home and he heard Lydia's voice raised in complaint.

He pushed them from his mind, and rang the doorbell, having checked the name on the plaque.

CHAPTER 14

"May I see Mr. Hayes, please?"

The maid opened the door a little wider. "Do you have an appointment, sir?"

Mr. Darcy shook his head. "No, I am making a general enquiry. I will not keep him many minutes."

She showed him into a waiting room. "He is seeing someone at the moment. I will tell him you are waiting as soon as he is free."

"Thank you." Mr. Darcy moved to the window and watched Mr. and Mrs. Wickham walking away up the street. He hoped most heartily that he might never have to see them again — except, of course, giving Wickham the other half of the bribe when he had found Elizabeth. He would not think of failure.

He took out her portrait from his pocket, and opened the case. Elizabeth smiled up at him from the painting, her cheeks glowing with health and her eyes looking directly into his, a little tendril of hair escaping in front of her ear. He smiled painfully, he hadn't smiled properly in a long time. But he was getting closer to her.

Only a few weeks ago, she had been here, in this house. He was closer. His hand trembled with emotion. He needed to see her, needed to know she was all right. He drew a few deep breaths, and realised he had forgotten to eat today. He needed to remedy that soon.

The door opened, and he turned, seeing a stooping older man, well dressed, with an indefinable air of authority.

"You wished to see me, sir?"

"Thank you. You are Mr. Hayes?"

The gentleman nodded. "Please come through to my study."

He followed him across the hall and they went into a quiet and calm room. He had prepared his story, and wondered how difficult it might be to get the information he needed.

"So, how can I help you, Mr. ...?"

"I'm sorry. I am Mr. Fitzwilliam Darcy, of Pemberley in Derbyshire." He opened the portrait, looked down at Elizabeth, then showed her image. The doctor nodded.

"I am searching for a Mr. Soames and this young lady, Miss Sarah Soames, his daughter. Their family do not know where they are. We feel he has moved away because he knows he is very ill and did not want them to see his decline."

The physician's face was expressionless.

Mr. Darcy drew a deep breath. "We do not want to intrude if he does not wish it, but we are concerned he does not have enough money with him, and that his daughter may be in need of assistance in caring for him."

The doctor's face softened and he looked sympathetic.

"That is a noble attitude, sir. I fear you may be right about Miss Soames having difficulty caring for him if she indeed cannot afford a household staff." He looked concerned.

"I saw them here, oh, about three weeks ago, I suppose. It was obvious to me that he had not long to live, he has a tumour which is affecting his ability to take nourishment. All I could do was to advise them of the importance of preparing food which is nourishing and easy to swallow, and to arrange for the purchase of laudanum when his pain becomes intractable." He shrugged. "If he is still alive, I would think he has only a few weeks, certainly no more than a month, left. He did not wish to talk of that, and therefore I did not raise the topic. I think he knows, though, and I believe his daughter also knew what the outcome will be. She seemed very tired to me even then, and there is a deep sadness within her. I suppose she is very lonely, if he has taken her away from her family."

Mr. Darcy nodded. "She is a very responsible and caring young lady, and she thinks a lot of him."

"That was obvious to me," Mr. Hayes replied. "How may I help further? I do not think he will be able to travel to see me again, and there will be nothing more I can do for him."

"I understand, and thank you for your help." Mr. Darcy said solemnly. "Can I be assured that they settled their account with you, for I can ease that worry, if they still have it?" He reached for his pocketbook.

"No, no, sir. The account has been settled. Do not concern yourself with that."

"I am happy to hear it. Do you have their address, sir? I was only able to find you when an acquaintance recognised them when passing in the road. They have not communicated the address to the family, but I would like to write to Miss Soames and offer any assistance she feels that she needs."

"Of course." Mr. Hayes got up and went to a large cabinet, and opened a door. He began to sift through very many papers.

"I am most obliged, sir. And what will be your fee for this appointment?"

"Here, I have the address." Mr. Hayes returned to his desk and began writing. He blotted the ink dry and handed it to Mr. Darcy.

"Blantyre House, it is in the village of Denton, west of this city."

"Thank you from the bottom of my heart." Mr. Darcy tucked the slip of paper into his pocket with Elizabeth's portrait and opened his pocket-book. "Is ten guineas satisfactory?"

"That will be welcome, sir." Mr. Hayes bowed. "Please give my best wishes to the young lady, and I hope you can be of assistance to her. I fear Mr. Soames may be beyond help. I can only recommend as much laudanum as is needed to relieve his pain. But it will not be an easy passing to observe."

Mr. Darcy tightened his lips. His Elizabeth was enduring this alone.

"Thank you for your help, sir. I will hurry to find them and assist where I can."

They bowed and he took his leave, almost running down the steps.

"She is at Blantyre House in Denton, Reed.

West from here. I hope we are not too late, that they have not gone."

Reed had leaped down and opened the door. As Mr. Darcy entered, the man hesitated.

"I am sorry to intervene sir, but may I take the liberty of stopping briefly upon the way and purchasing a pie and a flagon of wine for you?" he smiled a little. "I know you are in haste to find out if she is still there, but you have not eaten for many hours, sir."

Mr. Darcy nodded. "And neither have you. I am sorry. Ask the coachman to stop at an inn on the way to Denton. We will have half an hour to eat. No longer."

"Yes, sir." Reed closed the door and climbed up to give directions to the coachman, and they set off.

Darcy's heart was pounding in his ears, he was getting closer to her, and he wondered how to find out what he needed to know without frightening Mr. Soames into running away again. But maybe he was now too ill to do that, and they would be there. He hoped that was the case.

An hour later they stopped at an inn, and Reed hurried in to get a private room and arrange for food to be served.

Mr. Darcy climbed down and went to the coachman. "Thank you for all the waiting around you're doing. Please get the horses fed and watered and find yourself something to eat. I will tell the ostler to charge it to my account. But we must leave again in half an hour."

The man touched his hat. "Thank you, sir."

Mr. Darcy turned and made his way into the inn. He told Reed to sit with him and eat, as he wished to discuss the best course of action to take.

"Perhaps, sir, you could enlist the help of the parish clergyman?" Reed was trying to think of ways to find out if the family was there. "Or maybe the local magistrate?"

Mr. Darcy scowled. "I have little faith in the clergy, having seen the recent behaviour of a certain odious example. But I will consider it." He thought for a while. He didn't want to frighten Elizabeth if she did not remember him, but he also wished to be close enough to offer help to her as soon as he could reasonably do so.

Thinking of her aunt, he drew out a sheet of notepaper, and hastily penned a short letter.

> *Dear Mrs. Gardiner,*
> *I hope this letter finds you and Mr.*
>   *Gardiner well. I have seen the*
>   *physician in the house that Mrs.*
>   *Wickham saw Elizabeth leaving. I*
>   *have from him her address as*

> *Blantyre House, Denton, a little west*
> *of Newcastle in Northumberland,*
> *and I am on my way now. It seems*
> *that Mr. Soames is very ill and likely*
> *to be dying. I may be busy trying to*
> *help Elizabeth get through this as*
> *best I can as soon as I arrive. If that*
> *is the case, I may not find a moment*
> *to write, so I am sending this back*
> *now so that you will know where*
> *I am.*
>
> *Should my news be any different, then I*
> *will write and tell you. You may*
> *write to me care of the post at*
> *Denton.*
>
> *My felicitations to you both,*

He sealed the letter and addressed it, thinking fondly of the couple who were well-bred and perfectly in accord with those he wished to know. How strange that Gardiner came from the same family as Mrs. Bennet, the comparison was odious. He smiled, and gave the letter to his steward. "Get this to the express post, please, and then we will be on our way."

CHAPTER 15

*S*he left the house and climbed the hill as fast as she could. She could not stay away long, but she had to escape the piteous cries of the man who depended so much on her. He was suffering such pain, and could barely swallow the thinnest of gruel now. She had taken it upon herself to give him a little more laudanum than the local doctor had suggested, and for the moment, her Papa was resting more peacefully. She had reached for her hat and told the housekeeper to sit with him for an hour while she took the benefit of some fresh air.

She knew it could not be long now until he was at peace, but that made her feel even more frightened. Who was she, really? And who would she go to when she had no one? He was so confused now that she knew he would take to the grave whatever knowledge of her he had.

She walked along the narrow path right at the top of the hill, letting the wind blow away from her the foul miasma of his sickroom.

A coach and four rolling along the road on the opposite slope caught her eye. She rarely saw any traffic and so she stood and watched it idly as the clouds scudded across the sky behind it.

Then she turned and began to walk further along the path. Poor Papa, he had been so brave, right up until the last few days, when his pain became intractable. She almost wished him free of pain now. But that made her feel most guilty, because partly it was to relieve her discomfort at having to observe it, and her wish to be free of the endless exhaustion of caring for him.

And something else was concerning her. She didn't go to her room now, she tried to sleep at night sitting in the chair in his room. But when her body snatched moments to sleep her dreams were deeply troubling. The tall, dark-haired man with the burning eyes was always there now, standing too far away to aid her, although she sensed he wanted to help. She would wake, knowing she was calling him and he never came.

She also knew a deep sadness for another, a vague recollection of standing by some trees, watching a funeral service at a small country church, tears running down her face.

Was it a premonition of Papa's burial? But the detail seemed too real. Whose funeral was it? It was too late now to ask Papa about her mother. Was it Mama's burial? But as she scanned the mourners in her dream, Papa was not there, although the tall stranger from her dreams was standing with another, some way aside.

She was confused and upset, when she had to be strong for Papa, and her mind seemed to be unravelling. She felt tears start to her eyes and she blinked furiously. Nothing was to be served by being weak and spineless. Although she'd been compliant and quiet when she first began this life, she was developing a sense that she had been different before. She was also beginning to get a sense that she was going to have to be very strong as this feeling of who she was continued to unravel.

She needed to go home, Papa would wake soon, and she must try and spoon a little sugar water into him. She turned and began to walk back.

She stopped in surprise. The coach had halted on the road about half a mile away, and a tall, dark-haired man was striding up the hill towards her.

Exactly like in her dream. She gasped, her hand in front of her mouth, and the man stopped instantly, still many yards away.

She knew him as the man in her dream. He was the same stranger. Who was he? She stepped back, afraid.

He bowed, not moving towards her.

She felt her heart beginning to race. Would he be able to tell her who she was?

She took a few hesitant steps towards him. "Who are you?"

He bowed again. "May I come a little closer?"

She stopped, feeling frightened. "I … I don't know."

"Then I will remain here." He paused. "I have been looking for you for many weeks. I know you are using the name Miss Soames, and I know you might be in need of assistance to help care for Mr. Soames." His eyes were familiar from her dreams. "May I help you, madam? I wish to help in any way I can. I was making my way to Denton to offer assistance when I saw you out here."

She glanced around, there was no one else apart from two men by the coach many yards away. She felt a little safer. "Who are you?"

"Darcy. Mr. Fitzwilliam Darcy. I am a friend and I wish to help you in any way you ask."

"Why would you want to help *me*?" She was

conscious of the time passing, she needed to go. But —

"Do … do you know who I am?"

He inclined his head. "I know you have many cares and concerns, and that it may be best for you to stay as Miss Soames for now. But I am here to take some of the weight from your shoulders."

The tears started to her eyes again. No one had showed her concern for many weeks. The staff expected her to do her duty, and Papa was now only eaten up with his own pain.

"I don't see why you would."

"I am a friend, I'll be here whenever you need me."

"Here?" She indicated the whole landscape.

He smiled, a slow smile that made her own lips curve in response. "I could be here any day, in case you may walk up here again. Or perhaps it would be better for you to send for me. You might not be free to walk up here. I will take a house locally and let the parson know how to find me. Then if you need me, you may send word to the parson who will tell your servant where to go to give me your message."

She turned away. "I must go." She knew Papa needed her, and if she stayed she might ask again who she was. Her mind reeled at the thought and she knew she dare not ask, not yet.

"Remember I am here to help, I would be honoured if you can ask." He sounded as if he did not want her to go, but he made no attempt to stop her. If he had, she would have run from him. Perhaps he knew that.

CHAPTER 16

*S*he hurried back down the path, unsure whether she was running away from him or towards Papa and her duties.

Darcy. Mr. Darcy. At least she now knew the name of the man in her dreams. But why had she been dreaming of him? And he said he was a friend? That meant she definitely wasn't Sarah Soames.

She could not think of that. Papa — or the man she called Papa, needed her. She would not shirk from that, whoever she was. He had been good to her when she didn't know who she was and she owed him her loyalty. But she wasn't Sarah.

Perhaps she should have asked the stranger

her given name. It was hard to think of herself as not-Sarah.

That evening, as she tried to encourage Papa to drink tiny sips of water, watching him struggle to swallow, his hand a claw-like grip on her wrist, she wondered why she felt nothing but pity for him, the man who had stolen away her past.

But she could not confront him, he tossed and turned and cried out in pain, and she placed a tiny amount of laudanum in his cheek. That seemed to soothe him since he could no longer swallow so easily. The endless hours of darkness followed and she lifted the compresses to his forehead, wiped the sweat from his brow, all the while remembering the conversation of the afternoon.

I am a friend, and I wish to help you.

Remember, I am here to help.

I have been looking for you for many weeks.

You might be in need of assistance.

I'll be here whenever you need me.

She felt a calmness, and much less alone. For the first time she could recall, she felt secure. It gave her strength, even though she was still alone, still had the care of Papa. She recited Mr. Darcy's words through the night.

I am a friend, and I wish to help you.

I am a friend, and I wish to help you.

It helped her so much, and in the morning she

was able to wash Papa with the help of the the housemaid.

He was so restless now, and she noticed his waxy, yellowish skin, saw his eyes fixed on her, pleading.

"All right, Papa. Now you are sitting up a little, I will help you to drink something." She held a spoon with a few drops of water to his dry and cracked lips, and he swallowed painfully. She waited patiently for his throat to clear before giving him a few more drops. Thus passed the morning.

As she sat in the chair beside him again while he slept, she realised she did not have to do this all herself. If Mr. Darcy really wanted to help, then she could let him without showing herself as weak. She would also be grateful of his help when Papa died, which she knew would be soon. She had not the least idea of what she should do, and he appeared to have no other family.

That sent her thinking of his property, his London establishment and the pretty little estate in Dorset. If Mr. Darcy could find her when she herself had not been able to find out who she was, then he would be able to help her find Papa's relations.

She went to the small desk and drew a sheet

of notepaper and a pen towards her. She glanced at Papa on the bed as she opened the inkwell.

Dear Mr. Darcy,

She paused, how did one greet a stranger who wasn't a stranger?

> *I have been thinking of our conversation yesterday. I would be pleased if you would care to call upon me at Blantyre House when convenient. I ask that you understand that the house is in some disarray, because, as you know, Mr. Soames is most unwell.*

She didn't sign the letter, unsure whether to use her assumed name and not knowing another she could use.

But she suddenly had a flash of memory, of brushing her hair in a bedroom, achingly familiar, and talking to a fair-haired young woman of about her own age, who smiled at her as if she was very close to her. Who was she? She trembled as her mind spun with *not-knowing*. What was she to do?

She sealed the letter and wrote Mr. Darcy's

name on the outside. She had no address, of course, but she sent it with the maid to the parsonage, hoping that some result would come of it, her heart beating faster with excitement.

Then she heard Papa cry out in pain, and forgetting both the letter and Mr. Darcy, she ran back to his room.

For an hour she struggled with trying to make him more comfortable, moving his pillows and rearranging the blankets. She spooned a tiny dose of the laudanum into him and gave him a few drops of water. But even that didn't ease him, and his thin hand grasped her wrist with desperate strength.

"All right, Papa, if you let go I can give you a little more water, just try and let go for a moment. I am here, I won't leave you," she promised, her voice trembling.

Then a strong presence was beside her and Mr. Darcy was there. "Let me lift you up a little, sir. Then we can help you drink something." With strength and a sure touch he helped the older man to sit up and she spooned the water in, drop by tiny drop.

"That's good, Mr. Soames. Let me help you lie down now and make you more comfortable. Do you have a lot of pain? Mr. Hayes, your physician from Newcastle told me only yesterday that a little more laudanum might be helpful to you."

Papa turned his eyes towards the other man, not questioning his presence there, and nodded.

Mr. Darcy looked at her, his gaze warm and concerned. "Let's make him more comfortable, madam."

She smiled back, feeling nothing but relief at the relinquishment of the aching responsibility and the kindness and skill of the handsome stranger.

"How does he take the laudanum?" Mr. Darcy took the bottle from the side table. "And how much?"

She moved over beside him, feeling his strength and health and the power of his personality.

"Let me, please." She took the bottle from him, feeling a jolt of recognition as her hand brushed his. She couldn't look at his face.

She took the bottle over to the bed and measured out the tiniest amount she could. "Here you are, Papa." She carefully tipped the few drops into the inside of his cheek. "There you are. You will soon be free of the worst of the pain."

He reached up and grasped her wrist, gripping with a panic and gasping.

"It's all right, Papa. I will stay with you." She

reached around and checked that her chair was there, before sinking into it, still held in his grasp.

She looked up. "I am sorry, sir. I had hoped that I might be able to entertain you more fittingly."

Mr. Darcy bowed. "I can see that you are needed here, madam. I would not wish to demand your attention while that is the case. However, may I order tea in here for you, and maybe something to eat? You look as if you have not eaten well for some time."

She glanced at Papa. "He has not been able to tolerate my eating in front of him recently. It makes him feel unwell. But I may be able to eat when he is asleep."

"May I order something to be prepared for you?"

She looked up at him. "That would be very kind, sir." She felt herself relaxing now that she had given up the control to him and she needed to make the best of it. It may not last long when he saw what had to be done, he might regret his offer and vanish again.

Once he had left the room, she leaned back and closed her eyes. But she could not rest. A spasm of pain caused Papa to dig his fingernails into her wrist. Wearily she rose and reached with her free hand for the wet cloths to soothe his forehead.

She was startled to feel his skin was burning hot. But there was nothing to be done, she continued to murmur soothing words and to change the cloths.

Mr. Darcy came back into the room and stood in the doorway. She found herself longing for him to come closer, she almost wished to lean against him, take in some of his calm strength. She swayed a little and he did step closer.

"Please sit down, madam, you must be very tired."

She turned and smiled at him. "He is nearly asleep now. I will have a little while then."

He nodded. "Who sits with him when you leave the room?"

"Whoever I can persuade," she said. "I think they are a little frightened."

"I understand." He looked at the dying man. "I think it may be as well to engage some experienced nurses. Then you can be the family he craves."

She looked at the bed, and shook her head. Slowly Papa's tight grip loosened and she laid his hand back on the bed, beckoning Mr. Darcy to the door.

The maid was bringing some hot water, and

she told her to sit with Mr. Soames and call her if he woke. Afterwards she led Mr. Darcy to the front door and stepped outside.

"Thank you for arriving so fast. I am sorry that he became so distressed I could not leave him. But it was — comforting to have you here. Your offer of nurses is very kind. But I fear it is too late for that."

He bowed his head. "I am sorry you are going through this, and I wish I could make it all go away. But I know that you wish to see this through."

She nodded. "He has been kind to me. I feel it my duty to be here for him."

Mr. Darcy looked as if he wanted to say something, but he stayed silent.

She struggled for the words. "He has always called me Sarah, but I have known that I am not her. Was there ever a real Sarah?"

He stayed silent, thinking. "I am not sure that knowledge would be useful to you at the moment." He drew a deep breath. "I have seen many specialist physicians about your memory loss following that accident. They have all assured me that you will regain it in time, but I do feel you have so much to concern yourself with now, that it would be unwise to push yourself sooner than you are ready to."

She looked up at him, determined on finding out at least something. "Tell me just one thing, then. What were we to one another that made you so determined to find me?"

He hesitated. "I am a friend of yours. I was about to ask you to do me the honour of becoming my wife. I heard later that you talked with a family member and were minded to accept my proposal."

She was very quiet for a few minutes. "I dreamed of you, these last months. I didn't know who you were, but I dreamed of you. But you were always too far away to help me."

His voice was husky. "I am sorry it took so very long to find you. But I am here now, and I will help you do what you feel you must do."

"I don't know you," she said, staring out over the hills. "I don't know you at all."

"We must start again, learn about each other." He didn't sound impatient, or demanding and of course she knew things about him already. He was patient, skilled with the sick, infinitely caring. And he had promised to help her.

Exhaustion came upon her again, suddenly, in the way it always did now. She pushed herself away from the wall where she'd been leaning.

"You must go now. I will go and sit with Papa and try and sleep while he does."

He nodded agreement. "If I sat with him, would you be able to go to bed?"

She shook her head. "I do not think we have much longer together. I will stay with him."

"Of course." He hesitated again. "May I call on you tomorrow?"

CHAPTER 17

*D*arcy sat in the front parlour of the small and ill-favoured cottage he had rented in Denton. Its only recommendation was that it was instantly available and it was close to Blantyre House.

Exhaustion swept over him now that the long separation was over. He had found her. Now Mr. Soames was beyond concealing her and he would not lose her again.

He stretched. He would not go to bed tonight, he would sit up and wait for the call. He doubted Mr. Soames would live through the night, and he expected she would call for him.

He drew a sheet of notepaper towards him. He would write to Mrs. Gardiner, and tell her everything that Elizabeth had gone through and how loyal and dedicated she was being. But also that she did not appear to remember anything at all, she had not asked about her family. He put the pen down and frowned. Surely most young women would ask if they had a family?

Something wasn't right. He shook his head. He would not write just yet. Perhaps she was just so exhausted with the strain of nursing Soames she had not time to think.

He went to the door. "Mr. Reed!"

His steward appeared. "Yes, sir?"

"I have told you the situation at Blantyre House. But I have an uneasy feeling this evening. Please go and wait near the house in case you are needed. Take a cab and retain it to be with you there. It will give you somewhere to sit."

"Yes, sir." Reed did not demur, or ask what he was concerned about. He was a good man, and Darcy determined to reward him when he got home to Pemberley — with Elizabeth.

He smiled a little to himself as he went back into the house. He thought of her as Elizabeth now, not Miss Bennet. He must try and remember she was a different person now in her own mind. He must court her again, help this new person learn to accept him.

He stretched out in the chair, he needed to

sleep. Tomorrow might be difficult for her. He must be ready to help.

HE WAS AWAKENED by shouting and a hammering on the door. He was instantly awake, but the noise didn't sound as he was expecting. The candles were still lit in the hall and the housekeeper rushed to the door. He squinted at the tall clock in the corner, it was three o'clock. What could it be? He hurried through.

The cabbie was at the door. "Hurry, sir."

Darcy took off to the cab at the end of the path, where he could see a struggle going on in the faint moonlight.

When he reached there, he saw Reed hanging onto a smaller man who was fighting to get away from him. Darcy grabbed at his collar.

"Stop it at once!" He used all the crackling authority he could muster. The man hesitated for a moment before resuming struggling. Darcy couldn't wait to allow gentlemanly behaviour to win out. He cuffed the man hard enough to make him shake his head groggily.

"What's he done, Reed?"

"It's Soames' steward, sir. He tried to take Miss Bennet away in their coach. He was trying to drag her and she was fighting him and crying, sir."

Darcy swore, and hit out at the man again. "You!" he barked at the cabbie. "Five guineas if you assist my steward and hold him."

The cabbie was suddenly filled with enthusiasm to get involved, and jumped to help.

Mr. Darcy turned and called to the housekeeper. "Send the coachman for the constable. At once!"

He turned back to Reed. "Press whatever charges we can get so this man is locked up until I get back. I must go to Blantyre House."

Reed looked wretched. "She ran, sir. I saw her running for the hill."

Soames must be dead. Darcy felt an unreasoning rage rise up against the man in front of him, but he didn't have time for that. He took off running, thankful that the cottage was not far from their house.

He was hardly dressed for running though, and he loosened his cravat as he went. He was glad he'd not gone to bed, that had saved many minutes.

He swung into the grounds of Blantyre House. All the servants were spilled out on the driveway and he heard the agonised cries of the dying man from within the house.

"For heaven's sake!" He identified the house-keeper. "You! Send someone right now to sit with your master. What are you thinking of, woman?"

He swung around and saw the driver of a coach. "You! What did you see? Tell me quickly!"

The coachman cringed away. "Mr. Fuller ordered the coach, sir. He told me he was going to Scotland."

"God!" he swung around to the staff. "Who saw where the young lady went? Who tried to help her?"

They all stared at him in shock and silence. The housekeeper stepped forward, nervously.

"Mr. Fuller said he was acting on Mr. Soames' orders, sir. We were to do as he said."

Mr. Darcy tried to control his feelings. He had to get them on his side. "So, did you see where the young lady went? Did she have anything with her? What was her state of mind?"

The housekeeper wrung her hands. "She was crying, sir. She was calling out that she had to stay with her Papa. She didn't want to get in the coach. Then another man who was sitting in a cab outside came running in and pulled him away from her. He told her to go back inside, but she stared at him and then ran out to the hill, sir. I think she often goes there to think and calm herself before coming back to Mr. Soames."

Darcy went to the gate and peered upwards. The visibility was not very good, the moon wasn't full enough for that and the clouds were quite thick.

"Which way did she go? Did you see?"

The woman came up beside him. "That path there, sir." She pointed out the way.

He turned and looked at her. "Thank you. Now make sure your master has some laudanum for the pain. Tell him she'll be back very shortly. Make sure someone stays with him. That is important."

She curtsied. "Yes, sir. Thank you."

He had an idea. "My steward will be here shortly to take over. You will do as he instructs."

"Yes, sir."

He went through the gate and started up the path.

CHAPTER 18

*F*ear drove her to run and run, her breath rasping in her throat, always upwards. She was sure he was not very fit, and she must outrun him. When she'd felt his strong grip on her wrist, she had fought with every fibre of her being.

She was so glad that she knew this path well, the occasional moonlight was all she needed to keep her safely on the path. A few minutes later, she risked a look behind her. Nothing. Perhaps she was safe. She slowed to a fast walk, hurrying to get up and around the shoulder of the hill so she could not be seen from the valley.

When she rounded that, it was nearly half an hour after she'd run from the house. She glanced back for a last look, she could see the staff running around on the drive in the flickering and flare of torches. The mysterious man in the cab had gone and the cab with him. He'd told her to go back in the house, even as he pulled Fuller off her. But she had been too frightened. No sooner had she been free than she started running. She'd be safe up here. She could think.

Papa. Poor Papa. She knew there was not much longer, and now she might not see him again. But he could still cry out loudly in his pain, so he would probably not die just yet. She wondered how she knew that.

Up around the hill and out of sight from everyone, she saw the place where she'd first seen Mr. Darcy's coach. She stared at the empty road. She thought she'd recognised the man who'd saved her from Fuller. Had he not been one of the men who'd stayed by the coach when Mr. Darcy had approached her then and spoken to her? She thought it might be, but she could not be sure. So she had to run. She needed to be sure, or rely only on herself.

She slowed right down, wishing that his coach would come around the road and into view again. But of course it didn't, and she turned along the path a bit longer. Then, glancing around to make sure she wasn't seen, she turned off the path and picked her way across the hillside towards a small cleft. Down there, a week or so ago, she'd found a tiny unused shepherd's hut, its door swinging open and she'd climbed in, feeling enclosed and safe.

That's where she was heading now. She could stop and think. No one, no one at all, would find her and she could gather her thoughts and decide what to do.

She felt a little wistful that Mr. Darcy wouldn't find her either, she almost wished he might. But if she left a trail for him, then Fuller might also find her, and she shuddered at the thought.

Her mind went back, unbidden, as she had sat beside Papa, and Mr. Fuller came to the door and beckoned to her.

She'd gone out to him, of course she had. Papa had trusted him and he'd been with Papa all along.

"Right," he'd said to her. "Your Papa has given me his instructions. He's given me money and I am to take you to Scotland. We're going to be married and do what he wanted."

She'd stared at him in shock. "I'm not going to Scotland. Papa wants me to stay here with him, and that's what I'm doing."

"You're coming with me," Fuller hissed viciously. "I was going to wait until he'd passed, of course I was, but that stranger with his proud and disdainful manner will stop all my plans. So we

..." and he grabbed her wrist, " ... are going to Scotland. Now."

"I won't!" she'd struggled to free her wrist and he'd tightened his grip painfully.

"You will, my proud little lady. You're going to be my wife, and you'll soon mend your ways."

Her heart had swollen in terror and she'd struggled as he dragged her from the house. "No, please. No! I want to stay with Papa! He needs me!"

She trembled again as she remembered, hurrying along the path, her memories speeding up her walk to a half-run.

She wished Mr. Darcy was with her. Then she'd be safe.

She reached the little hut and climbed up into it, and it rocked on its rusty wheels. It made her smile, even in her sadness, it was so tiny and so sweet. She peeped out of the window, it was still very dark, the half-moon high in the sky, with clouds sweeping across it. She shivered a little with tiredness.

She couldn't be with Papa, and she couldn't hear him either. She prayed that the housekeeper would look after him and sit with him and tell him she'd be back soon. But right now, there was nothing she could do to help him, and she curled up on the old, musty blankets on the built-in bench bed, and let the weariness overtake her.

Eyes shut, she began dreaming of Mr. Darcy even before sleep had overtaken her. Had he really wanted to marry her? She'd be safe if he did, safe from people like Fuller.

She craved the feeling of safety and security. If she was Mrs. Darcy she wouldn't have to worry who she was, would she?

She wondered who the fair-haired beautiful girl in that flash of memory was. Was she family? Would she have to get to know everyone all over again? She felt exhausted and frightened at the thought.

She must push all that away, push those worries to the back of her mind, and rest. Tomorrow she must go back to Blantyre House, back to her Papa. She did not know whether she would have to face Fuller, or what he would do if she did. Perhaps she could find Mr. Darcy and ask for his help when she first went back there.

She felt ashamed of having run away. She ought to face her problems, not run from them, but she didn't know what her problems were. How did you face an unknown past, full of people who knew who you were? Fuller had been there, the very first day. He must have helped Papa take her to their house in London. So he must know who she was, that she wasn't Sarah.

The questions circled her brain, making her head ache, until she could think no more, and fell into an uneasy sleep.

~

It was many hours later when she woke, still feeling tired and dull.

She got to her feet and stretched, knowing she had to go out at least as far as the stream, she was so thirsty.

She peered out of the tiny window. It was only just dawn. Perhaps she'd be safer if she went out now. The stream wasn't far. Having thought of that, she jumped to her feet and cautiously left the hut. She hurried to the stream and drank deeply before splashing her face.

Perhaps she should go back to Papa now. She stood, gazing further down the valley, drawing great breaths of fresh dawn air. Yes, she must go back, and she began climbing up past the hut, to the hill.

But as she came up over the hill, she saw dozens of men and dogs combing the hillside. She ducked back down in fear. Who were they looking for? It couldn't be her, could it?

In a frenzy of fear she ran back to the hut, hoping the prickling feeling on her shoulders wasn't because she had been observed. She shut and latched the door, happy at the sudden sense of safety, but concerned that it was not real security.

She thought back. She hadn't been seen, she was sure, she'd only been visible for a fraction of a moment, and anyway, they couldn't be looking for her. Why would they look for her?

Perhaps they were hunting Fuller. Maybe the strange man had gone to the police but Fuller had escaped. If he was on this hillside with her, she must hide.

She stared wildly around the hut. Maybe she'd put herself in a trap? She listened for a shout or the bark of a dog. But there was nothing. Silence. What should she do? What was going to happen to her?

CHAPTER 19

*M*r. Darcy urgently waved the men back. He'd seen her in just that instant as she'd rounded the top of the hill, but the sight of the searchers must have terrified her and he regretted allowing the constable to arrange a search.

"You must permit this, sir," he had said in his slow, Northern accent. "These hills are dangerous at night and she is a lady alone who has been grievously used."

The magistrate had nodded ponderously and since Mr. Darcy needed him to agree to imprison Fuller until charges could be brought, he'd agreed reluctantly to the search.

But the moment he'd seen her disappear back down the slope, he knew he had to stop this.

"Call them back!" he shouted at the constable, who forgot his authority enough to shrill on the whistle, and the men looked and fell back as they saw Darcy wave.

He bounded up the slope, and spoke to the man who was closest to the place where she'd been. "Where did she go?"

"Down there, sir. There's an old shepherd's hut there. I'd wager she spent the night in it."

"Thank you." Mr. Darcy began striding down the slope, hoping against hope she would forgive him for her fright this morning. But he'd never have found her this far off the path.

He'd spent several hours on the hill in the early hours, before going wearily back to the house to see if she'd returned and finding only the constable and magistrate there, both very full of self-importance at this event that had rocked the usual torpor of the place.

But now he was close to her again. He scanned the valley, not seeing her. She must be in this hut, and he must go in and help her, however angry with him she was.

He hesitated at the door. But he must not wait. If she was not here, he would waste time by waiting.

He knocked, and heard a startled cry.

"It is me, Mr. Darcy, madam. I want to help.

Mr. Fuller has been imprisoned, you are quite safe."

He waited, but there was no response. Maybe she didn't wish to see him. His heart twisted. He could not bear that she would be in fear of him.

"Madam?" No, he had to use that name, the one she had been taken for. "Miss Soames? I need to know you are all right. Then I will leave you if that is what you wish."

The door didn't open, but he could hear heart-wrenching sobbing from inside. He needed no other invitation. He unlatched the door and pushed his way in. She was crouched on the bench, her head in her hands.

"Oh, my dear! Please don't. I cannot bear it." He dropped to his knees in front of her, his arms aching to hold her, to comfort her.

Then, in an instant, she threw herself into his arms and he wrapped them around her, his heart both breaking at her pain, and swelling with love that she came to him for comfort.

They stayed like that for many minutes, then she pushed herself away from him, and turned away. He let her go, he must, but it was the hardest thing he had ever done.

"I'm sorry, I shouldn't have done that." Her voice was very small and tiny.

"I am happy that you still feel you can trust me. Here." He held out his handkerchief for her.

"Thank you." She took the fine linen square, and mopped at her eyes. She looked at him, then. "Thank you for finding me. I shouldn't have run away, it is not a brave thing to do."

"You were frightened. That odious man tried to take you against your will from everything you know, and you know there is still more you don't understand."

She shuddered. "He was going to force me to marry him. Then I could never escape."

"I know. Please, let me stay near you and protect you until you are settled somewhere safe." His voice broke, he could not ask her to marry him now, she would feel it to be a trap.

There was a shout outside, and he felt her tense.

"It is all right, I think the constable may wish to reassure himself of your safety. It was he that insisted on the search party."

"Oh, of course." She sounded nervous.

"It is all right. I will be with you." Mr. Darcy stood up. "I will go and reassure him, but he will wish to speak with you."

"I understand." She began patting her hair and smoothing down her skirts. He smiled at that, and went to the door, going carefully down the steps.

He nodded at the constable, who was panting down towards them. He must be angry that Darcy had not waited for him. He must appease him.

"Thank you for arranging the search. I would not have found this hut without it."

"I must speak to the young lady." The constable didn't quite dare to glare at him, but he couldn't hide that he wished to.

"Of course, she knows that, and ... oh, here she is." He turned and held out his hand to act as a support for her as she came down the steps, head high.

"Good morning, constable. I am so sorry to have put you and your men to such trouble."

Mr. Darcy had to clench his jaw not to laugh. This was his old Elizabeth coming back. With one brief sentence she'd taken the man all aback.

"Madam, I am happy that you are safe and well." The man hesitated. "Are you content for Mr. Darcy to remain with you? If you would prefer a woman to be in your company I can arrange ..."

"No, thank you. I am indebted to Mr. Darcy for his kindness and concern. It was the other man, Mr. Fuller, that tried to force me into the coach." She shuddered.

"Do not worry about him, Miss. He is incarcerated while charges are prepared." The constable was ponderous in his reassurances.

"Thank you, sir. It is a great relief to me."

She turned to Mr. Darcy. "Sir, do you know if my Papa is still alive? I would see him if I may."

He hesitated. "I do not know. He was when we left the house several hours ago. But as you know, he was near his time. We will go and see."

"Thank you." She stepped out beside him.

"But wait, you have no shoes! Are they in the hut?"

She smiled, "No, they are beside Papa's bed. I had kicked them off for comfort when Mr. Fuller called me outside."

He couldn't believe his ears. "And Mr. Fuller was going to take you to Scotland with no shoes?"

"I do not think he was looking at my feet." She sounded almost mischievous, and he had to smile.

"Nevertheless, I will need to send someone to fetch your shoes."

"Sir, that will take so long. I will begin walking anyway, the grass is not too coarse and there are few stones if I walk beside the path."

He looked at her dubiously. Elizabeth's free and independent spirit was definitely coming back and his heart rejoiced at that. But it would not be easy to persuade her when she was decided on something.

"Please," she said. "Poor Papa is alone without me."

"Very well, we will begin. But perhaps the constable will be able to send a man ahead to bring your shoes for the last part where the path is stony." He offered her his arm.

She smiled at him. "Thank you."

They began to walk up towards the brow of the hill, and he tried to pick the easiest way for her. As they reached the crest and started down the other side, she began to tremble.

"Is there something I can do?" he was concerned.

She shook her head. "No. I am just remembering things. Little things come back to me now and then. It makes me afraid, because I do not know who or what I am."

He wanted to take her in his arms again, tell her of his love and how he would help and protect her always. But he couldn't do that, it was not the way either of them had been brought up. He could only use words, which were not nearly comforting enough.

"I am so sorry you have to go through this. Just remember, I will assist in whatever way I can."

"I know that, thank you."

Halfway down, a man hurried up with her shoes, and she sat on a low wall and put them on. "That is better." She thanked the man and walked on beside Mr. Darcy.

Her steps slowed a little as they got near Blantyre House, and Mr. Darcy bent towards her. "Do not be afraid," he whispered, "I am here."

She smiled nervously. "I just hope he does not turn away from me for abandoning him for so long."

He shook his head. "I do not think he has a sense of how much time is passing any more."

She thought for a moment. "That might be true."

When they reached the house, she went quietly along the hall to Papa's room. Mr. Darcy stayed close behind her.

He was lying quietly, so still Darcy thought he was dead already, and he reached out for her.

But she moved closer to the bed. "Papa, I am here."

The emaciated man opened his eyes and looked at her with recognition. He smiled very slightly and she took his hand and sat down in the chair that the maid had just vacated.

He nodded at the maid. "Tea and a slice for Miss … for the lady." It would not do to have her not eat before this next test for her to bear.

He stood close to her, watching. It seemed to him that Mr. Soames had been waiting for her, and was now going to relax and let go. At least he was peaceful.

He watched her as she sat stroking the gnarled old hand, her eyes on the old man's face. He was watching hers as if he had been given the greatest gift on earth, but then his eyes closed and he lay, breathing erratically.

She smiled her thanks at Darcy as he placed the teacup in her free hand, and encouraged her with a smile and a nod to sip at it.

It seemed like hours he stood there, behind her. He watched as she swayed and sat back in the chair. Still holding the old man's hand, she leaned back and dozed. He was happy that she could do that, and after a little longer, he too, pulled up a chair. It would be a long vigil.

The maid crept in and out with fresh tea for him at intervals. Reed put his head around the door and held a low-voiced conversation with him. She didn't stir.

The magistrate looked in briefly too, and waved away when Darcy made to stand. Everything was just waiting now.

Then he stood up and leaned forward, touched her shoulder. "You need to wake now, madam. He's going." Mr. Soames was barely breathing, just a slight movement of his lips as the air moved imperceptibly past.

She sat forward, and clasped his hand properly, her other hand smoothing his forehead. "I'm here, Papa, just as you wanted. I'm here and you mustn't worry about me. I will be safe."

Mr. Darcy swallowed. He hoped she meant that she would be with him.

CHAPTER 20

She watched as his breaths became slower and slower. Then they were no more, and he lay peacefully. She sat and watched as his body became just that. Her Papa was gone.

She was aware Mr. Darcy was standing behind her, and tears prickled at the back of her eyes. He'd waited with her, let her sleep — she glanced at the sky, she must have slept an hour or more, and then he'd woken her so she was awake when Papa died. Such a wonderful man, he'd said he would help her, and he had. She was so fortunate.

She patted Papa's hand and stood up stiffly. Then she turned and went straight into Mr. Darcy's arms, resting her head against his chest. She knew she shouldn't, she knew she wasn't entitled to do that and when she heard his breathing catch, she knew she might hurt him if she wasn't careful. But she needed him so much.

He let her lean against him, his arm lightly around her, no more than at a dance, and she listened to his strong, steady heartbeat.

Thud, thud. Thud, thud. Thud, thud. She could almost go to sleep again, listening to that.

Then she sighed and looked up. "Thank you." She smiled. "Again."

His answering smile seemed difficult. "I'm happy I could help."

"What should we do now?" she asked. "I am not sure how to find his family."

"It is too late this evening to do anything," he said firmly. "I will tell the maid to pack you a bag, and send my steward to engage a room at the inn for you. I regret I have no chaperone for you at my cottage and I do not wish you to stay here alone tonight." He thought a moment.

"I do not think it will be very easy to find his family and arrange a burial in Dorset in the time available. So we will arrange to lay him to rest here."

He looked at her. "Please do not concern yourself with anything. I will do what is needed, with the assistance of my steward."

"Oh yes." She remembered what he had done. "I must thank him for what he did. Mr. Fuller might have been able to take me if he had not intervened." She shivered again. "The staff did not want to help me."

"Do not distress yourself, you must be strong for another few days, then we can leave here and begin to help you back to your real life."

"Yes." She shivered again. This was just as frightening.

"I don't think I want a chaperone, I don't want to be on my own at the inn." She looked up at him pleadingly.

His expression softened as he looked at her. "I will tell my steward to engage two rooms at the inn. Tonight, I do not wish you to do anything which might limit your choices when you feel better."

She turned and looked at Papa, lying there. Then she schooled her expression, stood up straight, and turned away. "You are right. Thank you, I will accept what you say." And she walked from the room, happy that at the end, he had been peaceful. And he had known she was there.

LATER THAT NIGHT, as she lay in comfort in crisp, clean sheets, she contemplated Mr. Darcy, who would be sleeping in the room across the corridor from her. She could not go to him unless she was in urgent need, but his nearness comforted her.

Slowly, she relaxed. She could sleep tonight. She was safe. She thought about Mr. Darcy. The handsome man from her dreams was now near enough to help her. His dark eyes sometimes looked at her with warm regard. He seemed to understand how to talk to her, how not to frighten her about her past.

But now Papa was dead, and she needed to learn who she was, needed to stop being Sarah, and be … who? She thought back, and realised he had never called her anything. He'd used the word madam sometimes, but never Sarah, or Miss Soames, or even whatever her real name was. No, that was wrong. He'd called her Miss Soames once. Just once, when she was crying in that shepherd's hut, asking permission to come in. Even then, he'd not forced himself on her, but when she'd thrown herself in his arms, he'd not rejected her.

She fell asleep with the imprint of his arms around her from her memory, infinitely comforting, and woke, much refreshed, in the morning.

She dressed quietly, wondering how she would get mourning clothes, or even if she should.

Opening her bedroom door, she saw his door

was open and he was standing there, waiting for her.

"Oh, I'm sorry. Have you been waiting long?"

He smiled and shook his head. "No, madam, not long. Let us go downstairs to eat."

He bowed and gave way to her and they went down to the dining room.

She looked around, it was quiet and there were no other travellers. "It seems that not many people stay in Denton, or pass through, sir."

He smiled. "I agree, it is a small and very pleasant village. But not close to the highway."

He looked curiously at her. "Did Mr. Soames ever say why he came here?"

She shook her head. "No, he didn't. I have thought about it since, and decided that he did not want to be found." She looked him straight in the eye. "I believe that he suspected he would be found if he returned to his own estate."

She watched him as he thought. "I believe you are right. I was there within two days of your flight from London, so if that is what he thought, then he was correct."

She was amazed. "You went to Dorset?"

He watched her. "Yes. I thought he would be certain to go there, and I would find you. But it seems he was afraid of pursuit. And the only reason to be afraid was because he knew you were not his daughter."

She put down her cup very carefully, then looked up at him. "You're right. So who am I?" she clasped her hands together on her lap so he wouldn't see them trembling.

He didn't answer at once, adding a little cream to his coffee with intense concentration. Then he looked up.

"I have to admit to being in somewhat of a dilemma. I am concerned for your health and for your state of mind. From my enquiries with the top physicians about recovering from memory loss, it seems the best way to reduce the stress of such a recovery process would be to allow those memories to return piecemeal, without undue pressure. But ..." He stopped, as she impetuously began to speak.

"What ..." then she sank back. She wanted to listen. "I'm sorry, please continue."

"I'm content to hear you." He smiled encouragingly.

She shook her head, and he waited a moment, and then continued.

"However, not one of those experts could bring to mind a case where the person was taken from every familiar person and place and thus did not have any opportunity to receive little reminders from those around them." He smiled sadly. "You have been grievously used, and I do not know how to help you best."

"I don't want to think of Papa as using me like that."

"Then we will talk only of the future, madam. Today, we will arrange to lay him to rest, in the manner you feel most fitting. I will arrange that your belongings are collected from Blantyre House and that the servants are let go at the appropriate time."

He thought for a few more moments. "I will engage a lawyer in London, I think, to settle his affairs in a proper fashion. He undoubtedly has family who will be able to take on the affairs of his estates."

"I'm so happy that I'm not doing this alone," she said fervently, and he smiled.

"But, sir, I must know one thing. I have no name. It is hard to be not-Sarah."

He made a face of distaste, and she continued hurriedly.

"When I was in Newcastle, I was accosted by a woman who called me Lizzy." She shuddered slightly, the woman had not been one she might wish to know. "I do not want to know whether she is what she said she was." Her voice trembled. "But, is that my name?"

He was gazing at her with that wonderful, caring expression, and — was it love? He smiled gently. "I will be so happy to be able to call you by the given name I know you by — Miss Elizabeth."

Elizabeth. She sighed. "That is enough. Thank you."

CHAPTER 21

They finished their breakfast and Mr. Darcy held her chair for her as she stood up.

"May I suggest that you collect your hat, Miss Elizabeth?" His voice caressed her name. "We need to go to the house to begin to make arrangements. Do not be concerned about the rest of your belongings here, I will retain the rooms for the time being."

She curtsied and slipped up to the bedroom to get her hat. As she tucked her hair up under it, she wondered how long they would be here, and where they would be going next? London? Where in the country did she come from? Her mind swayed again.

It seemed the one solid certainty in her life

was the tall, dark man who waited downstairs for her.

She stared out of the window at the hills. He'd said he had been going to propose to her — at least the girl she had been before all this had happened. She didn't know if she could be her again, or if she was changed forever? Could he love the new her, or might she have to act differently in order to keep him beside her?

Because she needed him beside her, he was quite certainly the only thing she had left in the world, and she felt a terror of abandonment brushing at the corners of her mind.

Shivering, she hurried downstairs to find him and reassure herself he was still there.

He was. She breathed a sigh of relief. He came towards her with an expression of concern.

"Miss Elizabeth, you are most pale, perhaps it would be better if you were to stay here and rest."

"No!" she found herself clinging to his arm. "No! I wish to stay with you." She noticed what she was doing and forced her hand away. It was hard to stop her body trembling.

"I am afraid for your state of mind, you've had so much uncertainty, and your whole world must seem to be vanishing around you." He drew her over to a chair.

She sat down. "You understand me and how I feel, but I don't want you to think I'm mad."

"You are not mad, Miss Elizabeth, I'm sure of that, and I'll help you to feel safer however I can."

She wrapped her arms around herself, forcing herself not to rock like a frightened child. "I am ready for the day."

"You're being very brave, and I will endeavour to make it as easy and quick as I can."

She stood up, drew a deep breath. "I am ready," she repeated.

He offered his arm, and she took it.

"We will go first to the magistrate's home," he said decidedly. "He will be able to call the under-taker, if he has not already. We will arrange the funeral for as soon as possible, if that accords with your wishes?"

She nodded, not saying anything. She had rarely been to the village and never on her own. Fuller had always been there, watching. She suppressed a shudder.

"One thing I might suggest is that you arrange it in the name of Miss Soames. That is how people know you here, and it will make for fewer questions about Mr. Soames' character."

"Oh, yes, I would not like anyone to malign Papa." She was pleased with that idea. Nothing could harm him now, but she did not want unpleasant talk.

At the magistrate's house, he greeted her paternally, setting her down in a comfortable chair and ordering tea.

"Yes, I informed the undertaker to be ready for you to call in the near future," he said. "But I need to talk to you about making a statement for the trial of Mr. Fuller."

She shrank back against the chair, her heart hammering.

Mr. Darcy glanced at her, and intervened. "Miss Soames understands that, but I would ask that you obtain statements from all the witnesses first — the Blantyre House staff and my steward — and after that, then the constable, with a chaperone, could perhaps obtain the statement in the least distressing way possible from the lady."

The magistrate nodded. "That is possible, perhaps. It seems that we may not be able to make a charge for theft hold because the man insists he was given the money by Mr. Soames, who is, of course, unable to verify that fact."

"It seems likely that Mr. Soames was unable for some weeks to make a promise like that." Mr. Darcy's voice was polite, but cold.

"Indeed," the magistrate said. "But if we are

to try him for that, Miss Soames might need to attest that fact in person at trial."

She was looking up at Mr. Darcy, and saw his lips tighten. "We understand, thank you, sir. Now if you will excuse us, we will continue with the arrangements for the burial."

As they left the house, he looked down at her. "I am sorry about that. There will be much curiosity today. If you feel able to trust me to make the arrangements, perhaps you would like to rest in my cottage for an hour or so?"

She felt quite tempted to agree to that, but then knew she could not bear to lose sight of him. She dropped her eyes. "Mr. Darcy, I am sorry to seem weak, but while I would like to rest, I do not want to leave you at present. I have … " She stopped and took a deep breath. "I feel most alone when I cannot see you, as I don't know what I should do, or be."

"Then we will conclude our business as soon as we can." He didn't sound upset or concerned about her weakness, and she sighed with relief. She was angry at herself though. She must learn to be stronger, or she might drive him away.

They began to walk along the road, and they came to the undertaker's premises, pointed out to them by the magistrate. She saw Mr. Darcy's steward coming towards them, from the direction of Blantyre House.

Mr. Darcy stopped and waited for him. "Well, Mr. Reed, how is the household?"

Mr. Reed stopped and bowed to Elizabeth. Then he spoke to his master. "I am discovering about the place, sir. I have ensured that a member of staff is sitting with Mr. Soames at all times as a mark of respect. I have also ensured that the housekeeper now understands her duties more clearly. I believe she was perhaps wondering what might become of her when her master passed on." He chose his words carefully. "I have also been to see the person charged with the rental of the estate and arranged for it to return to their charge after the funeral. I will inform them of that day when you have made the arrangements." He turned to Elizabeth and smiled.

"I have told the maid to pack all your belongings and deliver them to the premises rented by Mr. Darcy for the time being. You will not need to return to Blantyre House unless you wish to."

"Thank you, Mr. Reed, you are most thoughtful." She saw the man flush.

"I also need to thank you for what you did that evening. If you had not been there, Mr. Fuller might have been able to ..." she shuddered.

"Madam, I am happy I was there. Mr. Darcy

sent me to watch for you, he had an uneasy feeling about your safety."

Elizabeth turned surprised eyes to Mr. Darcy's face. "You did not tell me that."

He shifted uncomfortably. "Thank you, Reed. Carry on, and I will tell you the date of the funeral once we have ascertained it."

They started along the path to the undertakers.

CHAPTER 22

"We should return to the cottage now for you to rest." Mr. Darcy made the decision as soon as they left the undertakers. Holding the funeral the very next morning was helpful, in that he could get her away from the village with all haste, but it was going to be very hard on her.

He wondered what she was actually thinking. At the undertakers, she had been able to state what she wanted for Mr. Soames, and make decisions without apparent distress. But her earlier statements had convinced him that she was far more fragile than her outer appearance suggested. He was concerned as to how to help her, how to get his Elizabeth back. He had already seen flashes of her, but mostly she was just very afraid.

He needed to write to Mrs. Gardiner and seek her advice. After all, she was family, and perhaps she would insist on taking Elizabeth back to London, to live with them and gradually recover there. But in that instance they would have to wait here for his letter to get to her, wait for Mrs. Gardiner to travel here with her husband, and then another three or four days to travel back to London. It would be another ten days or so, and all his instincts told him she needed security long before then.

Should he call for Georgiana, and take her back to Pemberley? He need not leave her at all, then, until she felt much more secure. He could call for the Gardiners, and later, Jane Bennet, slowly, as Elizabeth recovered. But by remaining at Pemberley she would come to be on familiar ground when she met people from her past.

Of course, what he wanted to do was to marry her as soon as she would accept him, assure her of his love and the security of knowing he was always there for her now, and she could know herself as Mrs. Darcy.

Despondently, he knew that she might be frightened away if he asked her, might lose all trust in him. If that happened, he did not know how she would manage.

"You are very quiet, Mr. Darcy." Her voice dragged him away from his thoughts.

"I'm sorry, I was thinking of what is still to be done to free you from any concerns."

She smiled painfully. "There is a tiny memory I have — of talking to, and laughing with a beautiful, fair-haired girl. We seem to be very good friends. Do you know who she is?"

He smiled down at her. "That would be your older sister, Jane. You and she have been very close all your lives. She is a very handsome young lady."

Her eyes sparkled a little. "I have a sister." Then she frowned. "That lady in Newcastle, she said she was my sister. But I have no memories of her."

Mr. Darcy cursed Mrs. Wickham under his breath. "You have four sisters, but you are very close to Jane. She has been most distressed since you disappeared."

"Have you informed her where I am?"

"I have told her I have found you, but the family are waiting until you are ready to meet them, perhaps initially by correspondence. It is very early days for you yet, since you are only now free to seek your past."

"Thank you. You are being most considerate." But she sounded very sad.

"If there is anything different you wish me to do, you must tell me at once." He was alarmed that she might not be happy with what he was proposing.

"No, there is nothing. I am just wondering if I am very different now, whether Jane will still like me."

Her matter-of-fact words tore at his heart. Did she wonder if he still loved her? Did she think she must be like she was before?

"I am sure you have nothing to worry about, Miss Elizabeth."

He was at a loss as to how to proceed with this, she had been through so much already. But his Elizabeth had a steely heart, where had that gone?

And his feelings angered him. She would never be the Elizabeth he had known, she would always have this experience in her past. He must love this Elizabeth, and help her to become all she could be of the girl he had loved. There was no one else for him.

They entered the small cottage, and he called for tea. They sat in the little parlour, and she exclaimed over the quaint furnishings and the tiny windows. He smiled to see her enjoyment, and they sat companionably over their tea.

Then she put down her cup with a sigh and nearly spoke, but stopped herself.

He smiled. "You may ask whatever it is you wish to," he said. "I will not be angry."

She smiled happily. "Then I would like to go for a walk in the fresh air."

He felt his heart lift. "Let's go, Miss Elizabeth. I agree it will be beneficial to both of us."

He waited while she put on her hat and picked up her parasol, and they walked along the road until they reached the path beside the hill. Her eyes turned to Blantyre House. "Perhaps I should go and sit with him a while."

"After our walk, we could do that if you feel you would like to." He didn't want her to feel obliged a moment longer than she should. He had been sorry for the man's suffering, but he still could not forgive him for what he had done to Elizabeth. It would remain with her for the rest of her life. He just hoped his own Elizabeth, strong, determined, lively and just a touch impertinent, would soon be back.

She nodded agreement and they walked a little way up the hill. Soon she found a low wall for them to sit on. They were still in view of the town, and he was happy for that to be so if that was what she chose.

She stared out over the landscape for several minutes. He saw she was biting her lip and wondered what she was diffident about saying to him.

She was still looking away as she spoke, and her face was suffused with pink. "If ... if Fuller had taken me to Scotland, how long would it have taken?"

He was astounded, he certainly had not expected that. "Would you want ... ?"

"No, no, definitely not. He was always looking at me, I didn't like him at all!" her face was pink and embarrassed. "I just wondered ..."

He was puzzled, there was something here he didn't understand. "We are not far from Scotland, maybe a long day of journeying, or two shorter days."

"Oh." She looked down.

He waited, he must be patient, he must find out what she was trying to say, he must give her time. He was glad that they were in sight of the village, or he might be tempted to take her in his arms. He must not do that, must not do anything to frighten her.

She bit her lip, her breathing was fast. What was troubling her?

"You know before, when I asked ... well, you said you had been going to ask me to marry you?"

He nodded. "Yes."

"Well, do you think, — do you think I might ever be like her again?" the words all came out in a rush, as if she was determined to get them said before she could change her mind.

CHAPTER 23

*E*lizabeth had to know. Would he, could he ever love her again? Or would she have to let him go? The thought of having to depend only on herself again was frightening.

He was silent and her heart sank. He must be trying to think of a kind answer, trying not to let her down.

His voice was very quiet. "Do you want to be like her? Or do you want to be you, and keep all the experiences you've had, and also regain the memories you've lost?"

He hadn't said he loved her. She felt herself sag down on the wall.

"Perhaps we should go back. I should sit with Papa for a while."

"Not yet." Mr. Darcy shook his head. "Something is troubling you, I haven't answered something that you wanted to know, perhaps I've not understood your questions." He touched her hand to stop her getting to her feet.

"If *I* took you to Scotland, what would you like to do there?"

She looked down, swinging her feet, which didn't quite touch the ground. If she told him, and he didn't want to marry her, it would make it too difficult for him to carry on helping her. She would be alone. But if he married her out of loyalty to Elizabeth, he would regret it and they'd both be unhappy. She couldn't bear to lose him, but also couldn't bear to force him to do something that he might not wish to.

"I cannot say."

He twisted to face her. "I hope you won't be offended if I use your given name, Elizabeth. But it really matters to me that I say what you need to hear." He looked as if he was trying to craft the words carefully in his head before saying them.

"I fear I may be too concerned with trying not to make you feel trapped or obliged to me, and therefore I'm causing you more distress."

"You don't want to make *me* feel trapped?" She looked up at him in surprise.

He looked surprised then, and if she hadn't been in such a confusion, she might have laughed.

"I assure you I do not, Miss Elizabeth. It is important that you have the freedom to make your life for yourself. It would be improper of me to seek to curtail your choices while you are so uncertain of yourself."

She shook her head. He was being honest, as far as she could make out, and she owed him the same.

"I do not feel trapped, sir. I feel — I feel unsafe, insecure, any time that I am not with you. But *I* do not want to seem to be taking advantage of *your* sense of loyalty to Elizabeth." She looked down sadly. "I am not Elizabeth."

"Would you prefer that I refer to you as Miss Sarah?" He sounded almost in pain when he said that, and her heart was full of anguish for him.

"No, I am not Sarah, and I never was. Sir, I am so sorry that I have caused you such pain, and that I am not the person you have been searching for."

"Do not be sorry, Elizabeth, and be assured I will never leave you to feel unsafe. Once you are more secure in knowing who you are and what you want, I will likely propose marriage to you — again," his voice was very husky, "and then you are likely to refuse me — as you so memorably did before."

"I refused you?" Elizabeth could not believe what she was hearing. "*I* refused *you?*"

His smile was twisted. "You did." He took her hand. "And I deserved it. But I have worked hard to become what you — what Elizabeth — wanted of me, and your aunt told me that you were now minded to accept my proposal."

She tried not to smile. "I think I need to have words with Elizabeth for being so disagreeable as to refuse you."

He did smile then. "What do you think Elizabeth will say to that?"

She tossed her head. "Perhaps she will try and assure me she had a reason, and perhaps I shall then say to her that the reason can no longer be considered appropriate, since she cannot remember it."

He chuckled, a deep, rich chuckle of genuine amusement. It made her feel warm inside and gave her a confidence she hadn't had that morning.

"If we are this close to Scotland, then perhaps Elizabeth might be brave enough to say that you might need to gain some courage to …" But she could not quite muster the confidence to say it. Instead, she changed direction.

"Would Elizabeth be brave enough to say that?"

He smiled slowly. "Elizabeth is within you. I see her occasionally, seeking to help you become brave and independent, as she was."

She knew her eyes were sparkling and for the first time she could remember, she felt alive.

Mr. Darcy was looking down at her, with a thoughtful expression. "I am still concerned that it might be too soon for you, Elizabeth, but I have to confess I am sorely tempted to make you mine and thus be able to keep you very close." He looked away, suddenly stern.

"I will find it very difficult to let you out of my sight for some time. You will have to be understanding."

"We will have to be understanding of each other." Elizabeth felt almost lightheaded with excitement. "We should be honest and plain-speaking."

"That is sometimes easier to promise than to do." Mr. Darcy looked around at her, one eyebrow very slightly raised.

She suddenly thought of something. "You mentioned an aunt. Does she know why I refused you? I might need to know."

He laughed. "I do not think your aunt knows. But I expect you told your sister. But *I* remember it very clearly, as you were — most open in earnestly informing me exactly the reason — and I am right here."

That remark silenced her. After a long time, she said hesitantly, "I do not think I really need to know. We are both different now."

A SHOUT from the village caught their attention. The constable was waving at them.

Elizabeth jumped to her feet. "What does he want?" The tremor in her voice showed that she felt hunted again.

"Don't be afraid, I am with you now. If he is ready to take your statement, then I will stay with you. And it will be good to get through it now." He bent so his lips were close to her ears.

"It would be a pity to have to wait here when you are quite decided to go to Scotland!" His warm breath raised the hairs on the back of her neck and she had to work hard not to sway into his arms.

Suddenly the fear of making her statement receded. How could she be afraid again, knowing he was near?

She would make the statement, then she would sit with her Papa a while, and finally, with the funeral tomorrow morning, she would have kept her promises to Papa, and she'd be able to leave here with her head held high.

Leave here with Mr. Darcy. Make a new life with Mr. Darcy. Suddenly the future seemed exciting again, and even knowing that she had to discover her past, and meet her family, seemed more exciting than terrifying. She picked her way down the slope towards the village, Mr. Darcy beside her, watchful she didn't stumble.

CHAPTER 24

*M*r. Darcy stood, head bowed, expression stern, at yet another graveside. It was early in the morning. None of the staff had appeared, their loyalty had not been strong and the previous evening, when he and Elizabeth had gone to the house after seeing the constable, they had found Papa's body lying in a deserted property.

She had insisted on staying there with him and reluctantly Mr. Darcy had agreed. He wanted to tell her that she owed Soames nothing. He had stolen half a year of her life, stolen her identity and put her in danger with his steward when he wasn't in a position to protect her.

But he bit back the comments, he loved her. He loved her loyalty and her strength to do what she had decided to do. And in another day it would all be over. They need never return to Denton, and it was only one night.

He had sent Reed to the inn and engaged a housekeeper for the night at an exorbitant rate. She had provided food and stoked the fires.

Reed had visited the undertakers and fetched the strong-smelling herbs needed and Darcy had suffered another night of utter discomfort.

During the night he decided that they would take two days to get to Scotland. A comfortable night at a top class inn would make all the difference.

But now they were at the graveside. He had told Elizabeth that he would leave Reed to guard her at his cottage while he attended the burial. It had not developed into a disagreement, but only because he gave way without too much demur.

"No," she had said. "I will go to the funeral."

"It is not seemly for a lady, Elizabeth."

"I know that. I have had a memory of another funeral, where I had to hide in the trees and watch from a distance. I was most grieved I could not be there." She looked at him. "I think you were there, standing a little aside, with another gentleman." She searched his eyes. "Whose funeral was that?"

He did not know how to dissemble. "I am sorry you only remember that part. It was your own father. I saw you there, and I wished I could have been with you then."

She had flinched at that. "I do not remember him," she said in a low voice. "Were we close?"

He nodded compassionately. "You were very close, I believe you to have been his favourite daughter, and he died very suddenly. There was no time to prepare, to say goodbye. I think you were very deeply affected."

"I will attend with you today." She had been firm and he could not argue. And there was no one from the family who would know, so the story was unlikely to spread.

So he stood beside her at the graveside, Reed on her other side. The undertaker, the vicar and the constable were the only other persons present. The scene was appropriately bleak.

At the conclusion, he turned away and walked beside her to the little lych gate, where she hesitated.

"Where are we going now?"

He offered her his arm. "We will go back to the cottage. I have arranged a late breakfast for you, and you can refresh yourself." After a night sitting up, she must long for a chance to revive herself.

"Thank you, that would be most welcome."

He was glad to be getting away from the

church. The sooner this whole sorry episode was over the sooner they could begin to build a new life together.

Back at the cottage, she went upstairs with the little housemaid to take her some hot water, there she would find her changes of clothes which he had had packed and sent from the inn, and he sat in the parlour, looking around him with disfavour. It had been a convenient place to rent, but he longed to be back at Pemberley, the large, commodious rooms, the comfortable chairs, the large grounds. Most of all, enough staff to meet all his needs and wants. He smiled. He had found Elizabeth, it would not be much longer until they were together at Pemberley.

He drew a sheet of notepaper towards him. He must write to Mrs. Gardiner.

> *Dear Mrs. Gardiner,*
> *I am sorry to have been a negligent*
> *correspondent over the last few days,*
> *but things have been decidedly*
> *eventful here. However, finally, we are*
> *going to be free to leave shortly.*
> *Elizabeth is aware she is not Miss Sarah*
> *Soames, but she has found it a very*
> *difficult time, and she has been*
> *through many distressing moments,*

not least, an attempt by Soames'
steward to abduct her.

However, during our time together, I begin
to see flashes of our beloved
Elizabeth and I believe her lively
character will be back with us
eventually. She has flashes of
memory, she has a small vignette of a
conversation with Miss Jane Bennet,
and she remembers watching her
father's burial from afar, although she
did not know whose funeral it was.

I believe that it is best to proceed very
slowly to allow her to recover without
too much distress.

I am a little at a loss as to how to say
this next piece of news, so I will be
direct. Elizabeth appears to think
that the only way to feel herself secure
is that she and I travel to Scotland
and marry there within the next
few days.

I believe that is the best thing for her, I
unwittingly caused her distress by
trying to stay distant from her until
she had recovered more, and as you
know, I wish only for her happiness.

We will then travel to Pemberley, and

*when she feels at home, then I would
like to invite you up to stay, so that
she can get to know you again, and
hear anecdotes from her past when
able to. Perhaps Miss Bennet might
by then be married to Mr. Bingley —
as you know, we both hope for that
— and then they could perhaps travel
up afterwards for her to renew her
acquaintance.*

*I hope that this plan meets with your
approval, and I am going to
encourage Elizabeth to write a short
note to you very soon. I have
mentioned you to her, and I believe
that you will be the best person for her
to meet first.*

*I will remain in touch and am, as
always, most grateful for your
generous and unstinting help during
this difficult time.*

He sealed and addressed the letter, and laid it
aside to send to the post with Reed.

He turned as he heard her footsteps on the
stairs, and bowed as she came into the room.

"I hope you will make a good meal, Elizabeth,
and then you will be ready for the day."

"Which is to …?" she smiled at him, looking fresh but still tired. They had both passed an uncomfortable night, of course. He smiled back at her.

"We are going to Scotland." He sat down at table with her. "I have decided that we will take two days over the journey, I think we both need the chance of a night's rest in a good inn on the way."

"Thank you, I think that will be a good idea." Her eyes fell on the letter but she was too polite to mention what she had noticed.

As they ate, he saw her eyes returning to it once or twice, and he decided to raise the subject.

"I have written to your aunt." He nodded at the letter. "I have told her that we are going to Scotland from here, and that later, when we are at Pemberley, we might invite her there for you to become acquainted again."

She looked anxious. "That is the Mrs. Gardiner written on the letter?"

He nodded. "Yes, but you will not meet her until you are ready. She is a kind, elegant lady, and you loved each other very dearly. She has been of great assistance to me during my search for you, and you could meet no one kinder on your journey to discover yourself."

She looked as if she was steeling herself for an

unpleasant task, and he decided to lighten the tone.

"But first, we will travel to Scotland. They have some wonderful landscapes to see and to walk through."

He had been right, her face brightened at the thought and she began to eat with more enthusiasm.

After half an hour, he excused himself and went to the door. He gave the letter to Reed and told him to also leave his address at Pemberley with the magistrate, so that any call for the trial could be communicated to them. He hoped that would not happen and believed he had arranged things so that she would not be troubled by having to appear at the trial.

He smiled at him. "Thank you for all you have done. I expect you will be happy to return to Pemberley."

"If that is where you wish to be sir, then, yes, I will."

"Once we are home, I wish you to have some free time, the second steward should be able to manage for a week while I am at home."

The man touched his hat and turned to do the tasks he'd been set. Darcy watched after him. A good man. He must make an effort to reward him for his loyalty.

AN HOUR LATER, he got her seated comfortably in the coach with several extra cushions. He'd hired the coach for an extra week so that they would not have to change until Pemberley and then the man could be paid off.

He'd been most offended on Elizabeth's behalf when he discovered how few clothes she had, how meagre her possessions. But what she had was packed away, and he had filed away in his mind to write again to Mrs. Gardiner and ask her to buy and send to Pemberley a full trousseau. He decided as well to ask her to interview for a suitable personal maid who was experienced and of high quality, to be waiting for them at Pemberley. He knew Elizabeth's aunt was the best person to undertake these tasks and she would be exceedingly pleased to be able to do something for her niece.

CHAPTER 25

*S*he looked over at him as he settled into the seat by the other window. "So, where exactly are we going?"

"A place called Otterburn tonight. It is in a very beautiful part of Northumberland, and I have been informed that it boasts an excellent inn." He smiled.

"Then tomorrow, it is about fifteen miles to the border with Scotland, and I thought we would go on to a pretty little place called Hawick."

She felt confused. "I thought it was called Gretna Green."

"If you want to go to Gretna, then we can do that. But it is further west, and we would take another day. But anywhere in Scotland will serve our purpose, so wherever you like will be approved of by me."

She could sense her face going pink, and she looked down.

"What purpose is that, Mr. Darcy?"

His warm, deep chuckle was closer now, he'd moved along the seat and was beside her.

"Perhaps you should tell me?"

She found herself swaying towards him. "That would be most improper, sir. I await your … declaration." She managed to stop herself from saying the word proposal just in time.

"I suppose now is as good a time as we may ever have," his murmur sent shivers of excitement through her.

He took her hand. "Elizabeth, I must tell you how much I love you. I loved you before you were taken from me. I loved you all those months I searched for you, and I love you now, however much you feel you are, or are not, Elizabeth." His voice was husky.

"Elizabeth, would you do me the very great honour of agreeing to become my wife? Will you allow me to help you feel safe and secure as Mrs. Darcy?"

She sighed, it was a perfect memory to store up in that place that was so empty now.

"Yes, sir. I will marry you. I have dreamed

about you and then you came and you've helped me. I feel I've known you so much longer than just these few days past." She felt tears starting to her eyes, how had she been so fortunate?

He leaned closer to her, and her heart beat faster. The touch of his hand as he drew her face towards him was like a shock of recognition, and she closed her eyes, her face lifted. The touch of his lips on hers was brief and searing and she swayed towards him.

But he lifted his head, and his thumb traced the line of her lips. "No, I must restrain myself, Elizabeth. Or I might take advantage of your consent to our marriage. We have not long to wait."

She opened her eyes. His voice had been thick with emotion and she wanted to see his expression. But he looked tight, controlled, and she felt let down.

"Don't look like that, dearest Elizabeth. We have only a day to wait, and I will not do you wrong." He smiled at her. "It is because I love you, not because you have done anything amiss."

She gazed out of the window, her heart still racing. What would it be like to be a married woman, she wondered? Would she be able to do her duty as mistress of Pemberley? Was it a large estate? How many staff would she have to manage? Would they pay her any regard? Her lip caught between her teeth and she felt her breathing speed up.

He took her hand. "Please do not worry about anything, Elizabeth. I would not see you anxious."

She smiled with difficulty. "It is nothing, Mr. Darcy." She glanced again at the wild countryside. Its beauty settled her thoughts a little, but nothing could take away the fact that she now knew only two people in the world — the man beside her, and his servant, and she had no place which was familiar to her.

She beat down the feeling of panic. "Tell me about your home. I wish to know what it is like."

He smiled. "Pemberley?" He was still holding her hand. "It is, in my opinion, the most lovely estate in the country. But I was raised there, lived all my childhood there, so I am undoubtedly not the best judge."

She gazed at him, expectantly.

"It is in Derbyshire, and the house sits in front of a lake in a beautiful landscape. We have all the most modern conveniences, and the staff are able to manage the property very well."

Elizabeth found her breathing getting faster. It seemed that Mr. Darcy was a wealthy man. Would the staff hate her? And who was she, was she well-bred enough to marry a man like him?

"Elizabeth, try to relax a little. Scotland is the place we're going and very soon you will be safe with me. Try not to worry about the future too much."

She shivered. "I will try. It seems harder without a past to trust in."

His expression softened. "We can begin to talk of your past as you feel able, Elizabeth. I'll attempt to assist you in building your past to make sense to you."

"Tell me where we first met, and when." She settled back against the cushions.

He looked down, seeming a little embarrassed. "I will tell you. But you recall I said that you had refused my first proposal? That was because I am afraid my behaviour was rather disagreeable." He looked rueful at her expression of surprise. "I will not hide anything from you."

He leaned back also. "You lived near a small village in Hertfordshire and a great friend of mine took a rental on an estate about three miles from your home. I was staying with him and we went to a local dance. You were there. I regret to say I felt myself rather above the company, and would not engage with the ladies and dance."

She smothered a laugh. "I can imagine that, sir! You have a haughty demeanour when you are angry. I have seen it when you spoke to the magistrate and the undertaker yesterday."

It was his turn to look discomfited, but he continued. "I found myself watching you whenever we met, and you were unafraid to tease me and remark upon my manners — or lack of them."

She gasped. "I was not so rude, I hope, Mr. Darcy, as to do such a thing! Perhaps Elizabeth should remain where she is."

He shook his head, smiling. "It would not be the reason to leave Elizabeth there. I was completely captivated by her lively manner and her independent thoughts."

She looked inside her. Would she be like that again? She must work hard to be more independent, it would be what he liked.

She was hungry when they arrived at Otterburn, and she took his arm and entered the inn with lively curiosity.

CHAPTER 26

*D*arcy stretched and yawned as he peered out of the window at the deserted Northumberland hills. They were rather bleak, but that was the way he loved his landscapes, untamed and deserted.

Elizabeth had loved the hills too, that was part of what made him realise that they were made for each other. And from what he had seen of this Elizabeth, she had learned to go into the hills when she needed to think.

Elizabeth. Thoughts of her filled his mind, as it had since he'd followed her to London after her father's death, as he'd planned and prepared his proposal, and ever since that terrible day when he feared he'd lost her forever.

He washed and dressed hurriedly, and

opened his bedroom door. Hers was open, and she was standing inside, looking out of the window at the opposite landscape that he'd been looking at.

"Good morning, madam." He'd never seen a lovelier sight.

She turned and curtsied. "Good morning, Mr. Darcy."

He bowed over her hand. "We will travel on after breakfast and cross into Scotland in the middle of the day."

She smiled rather tremulously. "Have I ever been to Scotland?" she asked suddenly.

"I don't know, although I do not think so." Mr. Darcy walked with her to the staircase and down to the ground floor.

"A new adventure then." She did not appear to be distressed by the idea, and in truth, she seemed very matter-of-fact about marrying him. He wasn't sure how he felt about that, and thought about it as they were shown to a quiet table in a private room with flattering attention from the innkeeper.

"You selected a most comfortable inn, Mr. Darcy. I have not slept so well for a long time." Elizabeth took a sip of her tea.

He watched her. "Can you remember ever sleeping well?"

Her eyes turned inwards. "No, I don't really recall it. I suppose it was a figure of speech."

"Such comments can help to make everything seem normal." He smiled.

"But nothing is normal." Her eyes were dancing. "Today might be our wedding day, is that correct?"

He let himself smile. "It is not how I imagined getting married, but, yes, you're right."

He hand went to her mouth. "I am so sorry, Mr. Darcy. I did not think about the family and friends you would wish to attend! Perhaps we should turn back towards your home." She bit her lip.

"Perhaps you have family who would not think it seemly for us to be travelling together as we are not married." Her eyes showed her anxiety, as if she thought she would be thrown out to travel alone.

He shook his head. "Definitely not. We are going to Scotland, and if you still consent, then you will become my wife." He smiled, "I agree it will make travelling together seem more orthodox. But I have only one relative who would object, and I care nothing for her disapproval." He had a mental image of Lady Catherine de Bourgh, and dismissed it instantly.

"The only relative I care about wants what

will make you happy, because she knows it will make me happy too. She is my young sister, who is waiting impatiently to have you come to Pemberley."

Elizabeth still looked rather cautious, but she was calmer. "What is her name, and have I met her?"

"You have met Georgiana, but only briefly. Circumstances meant that you could not go on to become friends at that point, but you seemed to like each other very much."

"Circumstances?"

He nodded. "Yes. If I try to explain that now, it might be confusing — indeed, it still confuses me. Let us go on to Scotland, and then we will go straight to Pemberley. I feel you need to put down roots before you begin to untangle the past."

"I am fortunate in knowing you, Mr. Darcy. It appears you know me better than I know myself." She smiled and took another pastry. "It is lovely to be able to eat without having to hurry away from table to my duties."

He nodded. "I am the fortunate one. My search for you was taking so long that I was afraid you would be married already when I found you. Then I would have to leave you — after assuring myself that you were happy and secure."

She shuddered a little. "Fuller nearly accomplished that — but I would not have been happy."

"Then I would not have given up. Somehow I would have got the marriage annulled." He leaned forward. "Be assured, Elizabeth, I will always be there for you."

She went a rosy pink colour and looked down. "Thank you." Then she looked up. "It still feels strange being called Elizabeth. But I am not feeling quite so much of an imposter with each day that passes."

"I think it is quite time to leave. Then you will soon be Mrs. Darcy and no imposter." Mr. Darcy rose and offered her his hand to stand.

As he turned towards the doorway, he saw Reed standing in the entrance.

"Is all ready, Mr. Reed?"

"Yes, sir. I just need the lady's permission to collect her luggage from her room, and then I can take it to the coach."

"Oh!" Elizabeth looked up. "Everything is packed already, Mr. Reed."

He bowed to her. "Then I will collect it now."

Elizabeth looked at Mr. Darcy. "He seems to be the perfect steward. Has he been with you a long time?"

Mr. Darcy nodded. "He has been with me many years. I watched him when he was first in the household staff and I took him as my steward from there." He offered her his arm.

"He has had a difficult time while I have been searching for you, and when we get home, I intend to give him some free time. But I do not think he has much interest in life outside Pemberley."

"I believe treating staff well must be important in gaining their loyalty." She looked thoughtful as they walked outside. "Do you think the Pemberley staff will accept me?"

He noticed the trace of anxiety in her tone.

"Please do not be concerned. I know that you have nothing to distress yourself over, but it will be hard to reassure you until you see it for yourself. Today, however, I wish you to enjoy our journey to Scotland and prepare for our marriage. It is a day that I want us both to be able to remember with satisfaction and enjoyment." He smiled down at her and her face cleared.

"Of course, you are right." Her steps lightened and he assisted her into the coach, and as soon as he was in and settled as well, the coach turned out of the inn and headed north.

CHAPTER 27

*E*lizabeth was beginning to believe the freedom of finally not having endless duties to her Papa, and from being free of concern as to who she was and what she would do once he had passed. The anxiety had been crouching in her mind all the time and she hadn't had any time to try and make any plans, nor any knowledge that everything would be all right.

But now she could push all her concerns away. Papa was at rest, Fuller was no longer a threat, money worries were unlikely to bedevil her again, and the man sitting beside her was all kindness and consideration.

She watched out of the window with a lively interest. "Will we be able to walk in the Scottish hills before we need to leave for Pemberley?"

"I will ensure we make time for that." He leaned across to gaze out of her window too. "These hills seem wild enough to us, but the Highlands further to the north are more dramatic and the heathers are most beautiful in the autumn months. We must travel back here next year and visit. Their beauty will entrance you."

"Oh, sir, that would be wonderful. Perhaps I might try and paint it. Although I am not sure what my artistic side is like."

He smiled at that. "You have said before that you did not paint or draw as you had no talent. But if your work pleases you and reminds you of what you have seen, then it has served the purpose for which it was made."

"If I cannot draw, then perhaps I should ask you to purchase a painting for me." She glanced at him archly.

"But then you might not have seen that particular landscape."

"But I am sure you would take me. We could walk in the hills until we found the viewpoint of the painting."

She found that he appeared to enjoy their gentle verbal sparring and made a note within her mind of this other way to please him. For she desperately wanted to please him and she was determined to learn how.

THEY CROSSED the border into Scotland at about lunchtime, but there were no visible signs of the change of country and the different marriage laws that now prevailed.

She had a sudden thought. "Mr. Darcy?"

He was leaning back in the seat just watching her. "Yes, Elizabeth?"

"Will I have to sign the register in my current name? I cannot remember what my signature looked like."

He sat up. "I know there is no register as such, but that is a very good point, Elizabeth. When we stop to eat and to find someone who can marry us, we will first find a place for you to practice a signature. I intend to find someone who can issue a certificate so that no one can later question our lawful union, and you will need to sign that."

At the next inn they stopped for a fine luncheon in a private room arranged for them by the innkeeper and Mr. Darcy produced notepaper and went to the table where there were pens and an inkwell.

She watched as he worked over the pen to make sure it was of a suitable quality, then he handed it to her and smiled.

"There you are."

She took it and signed her name several times, trying to get the words flowing.

"*Elizabeth Bennet. Elizabeth Bennet. Elizabeth Bennet.*" She tilted her head as she looked at the words. "One *t* or two?"

"One." He was watching her. "How does it feel?"

She wrote her name again. "Strange, but I have been rehearsing it in my head since I knew, so it is not too strange."

She handed him the notepaper. "Does that look like my handwriting?"

He took the sheet and scrutinised it. "Enough to suffice for the present." He folded it carefully and kissed it before placing it carefully in his pocket.

She watched openmouthed, before recovering her poise — even though she was aware her face was hot.

He chuckled again. "Soon I will need you to practice signing your name as Elizabeth Darcy."

A huge lump formed in her throat. This man loved her enough to want to marry her, confused and anxious as she was. Surely marriage would help her to become more like the Elizabeth he'd loved before?

The luncheon arrived, but Elizabeth could not

eat much. He seemed to understand even though he made a good meal.

"I am perfectly content, Elizabeth. Soon you will be mine and I will keep you safe."

After the meal Reed arrived. "I have two names, sir. Both of these men have been recommended by local business men of good repute, and both have showed me the certificate that they will issue. This second one is actually a churchman, so he might be better and more official."

"That is a good thought." Mr. Darcy took the paper containing the names. "Is this churchman free now? And how far is it to travel?"

"His parsonage is just around the corner. I have spoken to him and he will be at home all afternoon today. He seems a pleasant man. Even though it is not required, he prefers two witnesses, and his wife is happy to provide that service, and, if you wish it, I could be the other."

Mr. Darcy bowed slightly. "I would be honoured, Mr. Reed." Then he turned to Elizabeth, who was watching with interest.

"Well, shall we go and get married?"

She swallowed, it all seemed very prosaic. "Yes, Mr. Darcy."

He stood up and offered her his arm. "I know it seems very simple, but I have been thinking. The clergyman who holds the living close to

Pemberley is an honourable man. If you are minded to, I am sure he will hold a service of blessing for us when we get home."

"That might be agreeable, but for now, I am not concerned." Elizabeth took his arm and together they walked out to find the parsonage, followed by Mr. Reed.

It felt most strange to be walking down the road on Mr. Darcy's arm, ordinarily dressed, to go and get married, while all around them local people went about their daily lives, not even glancing their way. But she couldn't recall what an English wedding was like.

She looked at Mr. Darcy. "Have I attended a wedding before?"

He looked thoughtful. After a moment, he said, "I believe you attended the wedding of a close friend of yours to a distant cousin, but I am not certain of that. I was not in the area at the time."

"Oh." A few more steps. "What is the name of my friend who got married?"

He glanced down. "She was Miss Charlotte Lucas. Her married name is Collins."

"Thank you for telling me."

It was only a few more minutes before they were knocking at the door of the parsonage. An amiable-looking man came to the door and shook

Darcy's hand. He bowed at Elizabeth, who curtsied nervously.

"So, ye'd like to be wed, lass?" his accent was
so strongly Scottish that she had to strain to
understand him. Mr. Darcy squeezed her elbow
encouragingly.

She summoned up her courage and curtsied
again. "Yes, sir."

"Well, let's be getting on then." He turned to
Mr. Darcy. "Ye'd like my wife to act as witness,
I hear?"

Mr. Darcy nodded gravely. "We would be
honoured if you are both willing, sir."

The man vanished into the house and they
heard him calling. Soon they were crossing the
road to the little kirk, and she was standing in
front of the plain wooden table, next to Mr. Darcy,
his tall figure comforting and familiar.

Mr. Reed and the vicar's wife stood on either
side of them and the questions were simple and
easy. In only a few minutes, the words were
spoken.

"I now state that you are legally wed,
according to Scottish law." He produced a large
rolled certificate and filled it out with details given
to him by Mr. Darcy, who gave his address as
Pemberley, and Elizabeth's address as
Gracechurch Street, Cheapside, in London.

Elizabeth glanced at him as he gave the address, but she trusted him and did not comment.

Then she signed her name as Elizabeth Bennet, and he signed after her.

The certificate was allowed to dry before being rolled up and given to Mr. Darcy. Fee paid, the men shook hands and they all left the kirk together. At the end of the path, Mr. Darcy offered his arm to Elizabeth.

"May I assist you, Mrs. Darcy?"

She suddenly realised the hard lump of anxious concern that had been inside her for as long as she could remember, had gone. She smiled happily up at him, seeing his features softened with relief and pleasure.

She took his arm. "With pleasure, Mr. Darcy."

CHAPTER 28

*M*r. Darcy could barely believe his good fortune. He was finally married to Elizabeth. He cared nothing for the opinions of any of his friends or family, save Georgiana. And he knew she already liked Elizabeth and wanted to be friends.

They walked back towards the inn. He was especially conscious now of the light touch of her hand on his arm, and that the responsibility of his position was now absolute. He had taken this on willingly, but suddenly the enormity of it took him by surprise.

But Elizabeth seemed to know how he was feeling. "Mr. Darcy. Husband." She smiled. "Do you not think the hills suddenly seem to be brighter, more colourful than they were just half an hour ago?"

Startled, he looked out at the hillside. She was right. He looked at her. Her hand on his arm tightened imperceptibly.

"Do we have time for a short walk to enjoy the scenery?"

"If you would like to celebrate our marriage in that way, then let us do that." He turned and beckoned to Reed.

"Mr. Reed, could you take this certificate back to the coach and stow it safely in my luggage, please? Then you may alert the coachman and we will go back to the inn at Otterburn for the night. It was most comfortable."

Mr. Reed nodded. "Yes, sir."

Darcy and his wife turned onto a path that would lead them up towards the hills. He decided they would walk the lower path and just look at the hills today, because he was anxious to get back to Pemberley in three days, rather than four.

They found a small burn, the water bubbling over little pebbles and they crossed the tiny bridge.

"Oh, it's so pretty!" Elizabeth withdrew her hand from her husband's arm and knelt beside the stream. She cupped her hand in the water and tasted it.

"It is like drinking the mountain air itself, far

better than any wine. Try it, sir, I believe you will like it."

He found her enthusiasm infectious and, laughing, he dropped to one knee beside her.

"You are right, Elizabeth. Next time we wish to travel, we will return to Scotland first, when we have time to dally and see the scenery properly." He smiled. "I hope you will be fully well soon, for after Scotland I wish to take you to Paris, Rome and Vienna. All are beautiful cities which I think you will find of great interest."

He thought she was at her most beautiful when she stared at him with that look of wide-eyed wonder, and he drew her back to her feet. "We must go now. I am sorry to take you away, but I know you will be tired with the excitements of the day, and I do not wish you to be too weary before we begin our journey back to Pemberley."

RIDING in the coach back towards Otterburn, Elizabeth turned towards him. "You gave my address as Gracechurch Street, sir, for the certificate. But you know I was living at Blantyre House."

He frowned. "Yes, I did. You were living at Gracechurch Street with your aunt and uncle before you were taken after the accident. Your address since then was a fraudulent one. When you might wish to look at the certificate in the future, I do not wish you to be reminded of this time of fear, uncertainty and exhaustion."

"You are most thoughtful, sir. I am sorry if I angered you."

"Angered me? What made you think you angered me?" He saw her shrink back slightly and understood that his voice had hardened at the thoughts of her at Blantyre House. He forced his voice to be more even.

"No, I am sorry, you did not anger me. I was remembering how badly you had been used, and I was feeling angry on your behalf." He took her hand. "Please tell me if I forget myself and you do not like my tone of voice. I will not learn to change as soon as I would wish if I am not reminded."

He lifted her hand to his lips and kissed it. He felt her hand tremble. He must lay her fears to rest, even if it meant waiting longer to make her his.

"Elizabeth, one thing I will say now. We are married and our accommodation arrangements will now change. However, I want very much not to frighten or distress you. I will take two adjoining rooms at each inn. I will leave it to you to come to me when you are ready for me. I wish you to know that it is to allow you the choice, and not because I do not want you with me."

She looked down. "Thank you," she whispered.

RETURNING to the familiarity of the inn at Otterburn was a good idea. While she was refreshing herself in her room, he sat and penned two letters, one to Mrs. Reynolds on the changes to make at Pemberley. He had determined to close the public rooms and the park to casual visitors who wished to look around. That was not appropriate while Elizabeth was finding her feet and becoming secure there.

The other note was to Georgiana, explaining why he had decided to marry before returning to Pemberley and telling her more of how he thought Elizabeth would appreciate her friendship. Then he sent Reed ahead to go to Pemberley on the overnight express coaches with the letters and to ensure the estate was ready for them.

THEY SAT over coffee after a good dinner and

talked. Elizabeth seemed eager to hear of his childhood at Pemberley and what Georgiana was like.

It was some minutes later before he realised that she was keeping the topic on him and not on her own past. He smiled.

"And have you found any more memories returning, Elizabeth, that you would ask me to explain what they might mean?"

Her face lost its animation, and he cursed himself. Perhaps he should wait longer.

"No, sir." She was quiet a moment. "I would like to hear a little more about my sister Jane, if you are able to inform me about her."

He nodded. "You have been very close to Jane all your life. She is an exceptionally handsome and amiable young lady, with impeccable manners and ladylike behaviour."

She smiled, and he was thus encouraged to continue. "You remember I have told you that we met when I was staying with a great friend of mine in Hertfordshire near your home?"

She nodded, and he smiled.

"Well, my friend Mr. Bingley was captivated with your sister Jane, and I will tell you that you wished very much that they would marry, because she was as attached to him as he was with her."

He thought she looked lovely, her eyes alight with interest. "And are they married now, sir?"

He shook his head, "I do not know. I believe they may have waited until Miss Bennet knew you were safe. She would not have wanted to marry without your blessing."

Elizabeth sat up. "I had better write to her. She might be dismayed that I did not wait for her blessing to marry."

"Do not be anxious, Elizabeth. Your sister does not think like that. She would not begrudge you a moment's happiness. I do think that a letter from you might nudge her into accepting Mr. Bingley's hand in marriage." He smiled. "It would certainly make it easier for them to travel to visit us, without needing a chaperone."

He would not remind her of Miss Caroline's calculated rudeness to her, but he would not allow that lady to come to Pemberley for quite some time, although he could not risk losing the friendship of Bingley, or let him be pressured by Caroline to not allow Jane to visit. That would not be tolerable.

"You seem very thoughtful, Mr. Darcy." Elizabeth's voice drew him back to the present.

He shook his head. He must not think of the obstacles all the time. He had Elizabeth back, and they were going to Pemberley. Nothing else mattered. He smiled.

"It is getting late, and I wish to make an early start. Perhaps we should retire for the night." He stood up and offered her his hand. "First I must check with the coachman that all is ready."

She looked around. "Is Mr. Reed not here?"

"I have sent him ahead to Pemberley to ensure all is ready for us." Mr. Darcy signalled to the innkeeper, who responded with flattering speed.

"Call my coachman, please. I wish to give him instructions for the morning."

After he'd done that task, he complimented the innkeeper on his establishment, and arranged an early call with tea and a light breakfast. "These visits have been most comfortable. I hope to send you much business in the future."

The man bowed low. "I am honoured at your stay here, sir." And he showed them to their rooms.

One of the maids from the inn was there to wait on Elizabeth, and he bowed good night at her door.

He sat beside the fire in his room when he had washed and changed. He had to wait for her to come to him. He'd spoken to the innkeeper and the staff were all on alert for her security. But she was out of his sight and he could think of nothing but her safety and his fear of losing her.

He had to force himself not to seek her out. But a few moments later there was a soft knock on the interconnecting door of the suite he'd taken, and she was there, a shawl around her shoulders over her night shift.

He lost his breath at her loveliness, and held the door open for her.

CHAPTER 29

*E*lizabeth found herself gaining in confidence over the next two days as they journeyed to Pemberley.

Her husband was gentleness itself and most attentive and she found herself relaxing more as the days passed. And as she relaxed, the memory and fear of her time caring for and worrying over Papa began to fade. One day she remembered her home, and the name Longbourn.

"Is the rest of my family still at — Longbourn?" They were rattling along in the coach when she remembered the name.

He jumped at her words. "Have you just remembered that?"

She nodded silently, surprised at his reaction.

"No, the family is not there. The estate was

entailed away from the family to a male cousin when your father died." Mr. Darcy's voice was bitter.

"Your family were out the same day as your father's funeral."

Elizabeth gasped, memory beating at the edges of her mind. "Oh!" she screwed her face up, thinking hard. "I think you came that day with another gentleman." She recalled her distress and the hysterics of a woman within the house.

Her husband took her hand as she struggled with the memories.

"Is my mother taken over with her nerves?" she tried not to show her distaste at the sound of the voice in her head.

He nodded, his face expressionless.

She looked down, a feeling of shame. "Is their behaviour so unreasonable as that?"

He squeezed her hand. "You and Jane are the most respectable and well-mannered of ladies. Your father was a gentleman. Your mother and younger sisters, I fear, often caused you to blush with their thoughtless remarks." He put his hand under her chin and lifted her face.

"But I love you. If you wish to see your family, I will never stop you." He smiled. "And I will behave properly towards them. I never want you to feel you must choose between them and myself."

"Thank you," she whispered. "Did I know the cousin who inherited the estate?"

"Yes." He nodded. "He visited your family before your father died."

His lips twitched. "I have heard that he decided you would be most fortunate if he married you and secured the estate for the family. It appeared you had to be most brutal in refusing his proposal, because he could not understand why you would refuse something so much to your advantage."

She stared at him, trying to assemble the pieces flooding into her mind. "Is he a clergyman?"

"Yes. He had a living in Kent. When you refused him, he was easily persuaded to marry your friend Charlotte. I think they are now living at Longbourn."

"Poor mother." Elizabeth was silent for a few minutes. "Are my other sisters at home with her?"

She watched him as he marshalled his thoughts. "Your eldest sister, Jane, is staying at Netherfield, Mr. Bingley's estate, at his invitation. You decided not to go there with her and went to stay with your aunt in London. Your youngest sister was already married, and lives in Newcastle, as you know. Your other two sisters, Mary and Catherine, are living with your mother in a small establishment in the village near Longbourn."

"Oh." She was silent for a while as she wrestled with the information. He sat quietly, letting her think, his hand warm and comforting around hers.

"Why did I go to London and not stay with Jane?"

"You told me you wished to leave the neighbourhood of Longbourn and you would take the invitation of your aunt and go to London." He hesitated. "I believe you did not want to see your cousin and your friend take over the Longbourn estate."

She nodded slowly. A picture of Charlotte swam into her mind and a sense of their friendship cooling when she became engaged to Mr. ...

"What is her married name?"

"Collins."

"Oh, yes. You have told me that already." She sank back into the cushions. This would take a lot of thinking about and assembling into a pattern.

They drove the next miles in silence. But it was not an uncomfortable silence, rather it was companionable.

LATER THAT DAY, as the coach turned a corner, she suddenly started, and clutched at Mr. Darcy. "Stop! Can we stop?"

He rapped on the roof of the coach and it drew to a halt. "What's the matter, Elizabeth?"

She was trying to open the door to the coach. "I remember this. I remember this place. Where are we?"

He reached over and opened the door. But his arm on her hand prevented her from stepping out. "Wait until the coachman has lowered the step, Elizabeth."

Soon they stood looking out over the landscape. A large, gracious house stood within an extensive landscape, reflected in a lake.

"I remember this. I remember." She turned to him, standing beside her. "What is it called?"

He smiled. "Welcome to Pemberley, Elizabeth."

She stood and simply stared. It was beautiful, and seemed to be the perfect place to be calm and rest.

She took a step towards it. "I cannot imagine anywhere better to be."

He took her arm. "I'm most happy to hear it. But you must not walk from here today. Let the coach convey us to the door. Then the staff can meet us in the way that they would prefer."

She nodded, and turned to look at the house again. "Did you say I was with Aunt Gardiner the day I came here? An elegant lady, with light brown hair?"

He inclined his head. "That is correct."

"I remember her. I remember being here. I remember your housekeeper showing us the public rooms." She grinned mischievously. "She said how wonderful you were."

He shifted uncomfortably. "She's been here many years, and remembers me as a small boy." He smiled, almost reluctantly. "She has a forbidding exterior, but I always used to run to her with an injured knee. The nursemaid used to become upset with me for doing that."

Elizabeth laughed at the thought. "It is interesting to imagine you as a small boy."

He looked as if he wanted to be anywhere other than listening to this, and she turned back to the coach, thinking to change the conversation.

When they reached the imposing main entrance, several members of the staff were there. But Mr. Reed was there to come to the coach.

Mr. Darcy touched her arm. "I'm with you, Elizabeth. None of the staff will crowd you, or greet you until you greet them. I have instructed that, in case you were rather overwhelmed with the size of the establishment."

"Thank you for being so thoughtful, sir. I hope I will be all right." She glanced out of the window. "Is that Georgiana at the top of the steps?"

He bowed his head. "Yes. Again, she will stay her distance to allow you time to adjust to so many new people."

She turned her head and looked at him. "I feel at home already, knowing you are here." She forced herself to hide her shiver. *Please stay with me*, she said to herself. But she must be strong and not ask too much of him.

Then Mr. Reed opened the coach door and folded down the step. "Welcome to Pemberley, Mrs. Darcy."

She descended from the coach. "Thank you Mr. Reed. It is good to see you here." He bowed, and waited for Mr. Darcy to step down. As they moved towards the main entrance, the coach rattled off towards the stable.

Elizabeth looked at Mr. Darcy. "That coachman is the one from Denton, isn't he?"

He stopped and looked at her. Then he beckoned Reed over. "Mr. Reed, please stay with the coachman until the horses are watered and away. He is not to gossip with staff here, and can rest the horses when he stops next."

Mr. Reed bowed. "I understand." And he hurried off.

"I seem to need to thank you all the time." Elizabeth worried she was sounding repetitive.

"You do not need to thank me, it is what a husband will do for his wife without expecting any acknowledgement."

Her hand on her husband's arm, Elizabeth followed him to the house. She tried to smile and not look nervous, but she wasn't sure how successful she was going to be.

As they got to the top of the steps, she let him approach the young woman who seemed faintly familiar.

"Elizabeth, my dear, may I reintroduce you to Georgiana, my younger sister?"

She curtsied and the young woman curtsied to her as well.

"Good afternoon, Miss Darcy, I've been looking forward to meeting you today. I hope we'll be good friends."

"I hope so too, Mrs. Darcy. Was your journey very tiring?"

She shook her head, smiling. "No, but I'm very happy to be here at last."

They turned together to go into the house, but she hesitated slightly. She recognised the other woman standing there.

"You are the housekeeper here, are you not? I

do remember you, but I am sorry I do not yet recall your name."

"Mrs. Reynolds, madam. Welcome to Pemberley." She curtsied deeply.

Elizabeth inclined her head, ignoring the instinct to always curtsy at people and she tucked her free arm into Georgiana's. "I'm hoping you can show me how this house is managed, Miss Darcy. I will need a lot of assistance."

She could feel warmth and support radiating from her husband's comforting presence, and he led them through to the drawing room, where afternoon tea was set out.

Elizabeth went straight to the great windows and looked out. "It is so lovely here," she sighed. She sensed her husband coming to stand beside her and they stood quietly.

"I am going to ask something of you that might seem in excess of what is necessary, Elizabeth, but I hope you will agree because it will give me a greater peace of mind."

She glanced at his face in surprise. "Of course I will, whatever you ask."

His expression was tight. "Will you agree to always tell me if you wish to go out? I am uneasy at the thought I may not know where you are. I know it might seem confining, and in some weeks

I would hope to be able to trust myself not to fear losing you again."

She curtsied. "Sir, I will readily make that promise to you."

His face cleared. "Let us have some tea." They turned to the small sitting area in front of one of the great windows.

Georgiana was already sitting there, and she was pouring the tea. "I asked Mrs. Reynolds to make sure there were several varieties of pastries. Then we can see what you like, Mrs. Darcy."

"Please call me Elizabeth."

"And I would love you to call me Georgiana." The girl glanced at her brother, and he smiled as he sat down.

"Tell me what has been happening here, Georgiana. I expect you will be happy for some company."

CHAPTER 30

*H*e sat watching the two young women converse, both relaxing, and he allowed himself to gradually let go of the tension and worry that had been his travelling companions for so long.

Slowly, he began to think of all the things that needed doing now, to finish this task he had set himself.

Wickham needed to be paid off. But that would mean he would be gone from home for at least four days to get to Newcastle and back. He could not bear to do that just yet. But he would not allow Wickham to come here, so he would need to do something soon, or that scoundrel would anticipate his move.

He needed to make sure the security he had

set around Pemberley was enough to keep his Elizabeth safe, and yet not enough to attract her attention.

He needed to make sure Reed had some time to recover from the great demands he had placed on him over the last months. It would not be right to ignore the man's loyalty to him and the estate.

He needed to contact Mrs. Gardiner. She was the gateway to Elizabeth's family and he was cautious about approaching any other of them. But Elizabeth seemed to be remembering things sooner than he had anticipated, and the time might be right soon to invite Mr. and Mrs. Gardiner here to stay and help her remember the past he didn't know about and couldn't help her with.

Then he thought that he could drive to Newcastle and pay off Wickham while he knew they were here and she was safe with them. That would be the best thing to do.

He became aware that the room was silent and both the ladies were watching him curiously.

"I'm sorry, did you ask me something?"

Georgiana tried to hide her giggles, but Elizabeth smiled openly.

"It seems you are full of solemn thoughts, Mr. Darcy."

He inclined his head. "I think there is much to

be done following my absence. But that is no cause to ignore your company. I am sorry."

Elizabeth handed him a refilled teacup. "There is nothing to be sorry about. Georgiana and I have been talking about the estate. I was hoping she and I might walk in the gardens around the house tomorrow if the weather is clement."

He bowed his acquiescence. "We will see whether it is set fair at breakfast."

He saw Reed standing in the doorway, and excused himself from the ladies and joined him.

"Coach and driver off the estate?"

"Yes, sir. I paid him well, so he did not demur." The man turned to other matters. "There is a large post for you to deal with, as you might expect. I have put those letters that might be more urgent on the top."

Darcy took the sheaf of letters, and shuffled through them. "Thank you." He stretched. He needed a very hot bath.

"Tell Mr. James that I'll want a bath before dinner, and ask Mrs. Reynolds to make sure the new personal maid for Mrs. Darcy is at her post."

He went back to the ladies and made light conversation for another hour. Then he turned to his wife. "I have asked for dinner to be served a little early tonight, because you will be fatigued from your journey. Perhaps I could show you to your rooms now, and you may refresh yourself before dinner."

"It is a good idea, Mr. Darcy, I would welcome the chance to tidy myself."

"I arranged with Mrs. Gardiner to appoint you a lady's maid. She will be waiting to assist you. If you do not find her to your liking, we can arrange to interview another."

She looked surprised and he cursed himself for not raising the issue more delicately.

"She seems very good and very discreet," Georgiana said reassuringly. "I will go up too."

As he escorted Elizabeth up the sweeping staircase, she looked around her with awe. "It's so grand."

He looked around. It was home, and he had never considered that it might be very daunting. "I hope it will soon seem very familiar to you."

He showed her to her rooms, which adjoined his, suggested they meet downstairs when she was ready, and went into his own rooms with relief. His bath was waiting and he sank into the hot water with a groan of contentment, lying in the steaming water for many minutes, letting the ache in his muscles gradually ease.

Climbing out, he found his manservant had

laid out crisply laundered clean clothes for him, and he sighed with satisfaction.

"That is a most welcome sight, Mr. James."

Once dressed and ready, he went downstairs to the library and began dealing with the correspondence.

The letter from Mrs. Gardiner concerned him the most. He smiled over her hearty congratulations and felicitations on the occasion of their marriage, but his smile faded as he went on to read —

> *We are, of course, ready to make haste and travel up to Pemberley whenever you say that it will benefit Elizabeth, and thank you for your most kind invitation. As you may suppose I can hardly wait to see her again and assure myself of her safety and well-being. I need hardly say how earnestly grateful I am that you have taken such labour upon yourself to find her and how happy I am that you have reaped the reward you so richly deserve.*
>
> *However, I must warn you that Elizabeth's mother is most deeply*

*resolved that she has been deprived of
news of her daughter for far too long.
She is telling everyone that she will be
shortly making the journey to
Pemberley to see Elizabeth and tell her
that she needs to put the past behind
her and do her duty to you and her
family. In vain have I told her that you
are following the doctor's orders to help
Elizabeth regain her memory without
causing her harm, but, as you know,
she can be difficult to reason with.*

Mr. Darcy smiled grimly at the acute under-statement. He drew notepaper towards him. He had avoided corresponding with Mrs. Bennet and now circumstances made it impossible to continue in that vein.

*Dear Mrs. Bennet,
I am sure you will be most pleased to hear
that I have arrived home safely this
afternoon with your daughter
Elizabeth, and that we married last
week at the pretty village of Hawick
in Scotland.
Elizabeth is as well as can be expected,*

*given that she has been grievously
used over the last months.*

*However, I have been warned by the most
eminent physicians in the country that
her recovery may take many months,
and we must begin very carefully,
with absolute quiet here at Pemberley,
for her to gain confidence. Then, later,
I can begin to help reacquaint her
with her past, but initially only by
correspondence.*

*I will let you know immediately when you
are able to write to her, or else you might
get a letter from her, if that is how she
prefers it. Once she remembers you, then
we may arrange a visit. Until then, I am
to protect her and keep her quietly here,
where she may be well-looked after.*

*Please be assured I have her well-being
entirely at heart,*

Yours sincerely,

He glanced over it, it would do. If the woman turned up unannounced, he would have no compunction at arranging her accommodation at the inn in Lambton. He would under no circumstances allow her to upset his wife.

He sealed and addressed the letter and laid it aside for the post next morning. Hearing voices in the hall, he rose and went to the door. Seeing Elizabeth and Georgiana in happy conversation, he went and joined them.

"I think we are ready to dine."

The housekeeper was waiting, she curtsied at his words and the company went through to the dining room.

All through dinner, he could barely take his eyes off Elizabeth. She was wearing a different gown. It must be one of her old ones, sent up by Mrs. Gardiner, or perhaps a new one, purchased by that same lady. She looked captivating, and her eyes sparkled with happiness.

He found it a joy to see her so content.

CHAPTER 31

*A*s he walked around the lake some two weeks later with his wife beside him, he understood what contentment really meant. He had watched her relax, and gain in serenity — and he had done the same. She would talk to him of the past they shared, asking questions and trying to understand her past. He began to understand a little of what she was going through.

Still she avoided talking about when she was a much younger child. He didn't raise the topic, although he wondered if a slight encouragement might be in order.

But now the situation might arise naturally. Elizabeth was excited and anxious at the same time. This afternoon, Mr. and Mrs. Gardiner would arrive to visit them, with their children.

Mr. Darcy hoped the children's presence would be a good thing, but Mrs. Gardiner had become more anxious for their safety since Elizabeth's disappearance and had wished to bring them with her, with three nursemaids.

He knew Elizabeth had enjoyed entertaining them at their home in Cheapside, and he thought it would also be good for Georgiana to take her turn and see what sort of hard work having a family was. He hoped their uncontrolled chatter would not disturb the balance of Elizabeth's mind.

"So, Aunt Gardiner and I were close confidantes, I think you said." Elizabeth asked him again.

He inclined his head. "Indeed you were. I observed it myself."

She shook her head. "I think I have asked you that very often. I am sorry, sir."

He drew her to a halt. "Now, what have I said about you calling me *sir* when we are alone together?"

She made a face. "I regret that I forget so often — Fitzwilliam." She smiled. "You are most forgiving."

His face close to hers, he whispered. "You are my wife and I love you, Elizabeth." He could smell her light fragrance and his ardour increased.

She had come to him, very uneasy, the first night after their marriage, but he had soon understood she needed closeness and comfort more than any new intimacy.

He had restrained himself, he had waited so long for her already, and they had not fully consummated their marriage for several weeks. But now they were fully committed to each other and he was delighted at her unreserved passion for him and her eagerness to please him. His love increased with every passing day, and his Elizabeth was more apparent within her as the time passed.

She stepped out again, and he continued with her around the park.

"Will Aunt Gardiner expect us to hold a ball here, or other gathering for local people?" She sounded troubled. "Because I have also been aware that Georgiana sees no one apart from the family and wonder if that sits well with her?"

"There will be no entertaining groups of people here for some time, Elizabeth. Certainly not until I am convinced that it is what you want and are able to do. As for Georgiana, has she intimated any discontent with the fact that we do not entertain?"

"No, sir. It is something I have wondered

about, that is all. She has never indicated any impatience with her life."

He squeezed her arm. "Not *sir*. Fitzwilliam."

She shook her head sorrowfully. "I will get used to that ..." She smiled up at him, her eyes mischievous. "*Sir*."

He decided to ignore that and keep his dignity intact, and walked on, smiling inside. His Elizabeth was back.

THAT AFTERNOON, they waited on the steps at Pemberley as the coaches drew up outside. Georgiana stood beside them. Mr. Darcy was pleased with the way his sister had helped Elizabeth. She'd been friendly but not overly attentive, and had allowed Elizabeth space when she seemed to need it.

But today he was concerned with Elizabeth more. She stood calmly, head held high and he was so proud of her. But he could feel the trembling that she tried to hide.

He knew she had nothing to worry about, Mrs. Gardiner was a gracious lady who was very understanding and loved her niece. Elizabeth would be relaxed with her when she had assured herself of that fact.

Mr. Gardiner was a true gentleman, even if he was the brother of the dreadful Mrs. Bennet. He would not make any demands of Elizabeth, and he would stay in the background. He would also be under strict instructions from his wife.

Darcy watched as his footmen and stablehands hurried to the coach and the steps were lowered and the door opened. He thought Mrs. Gardiner might be as anxious as Elizabeth and he wished the next few moments were over.

And then they were. The ladies curtsied to each other and Mr. Gardiner bowed. Then Elizabeth indicated the house.

"Let us go through." She smiled as the children were marshalled together by the nursemaids who had hurried from the following coach.

The two men sat a little way away from the ladies and made small talk about the journey from London, but Mr. Darcy was abstracted as he tried to listen to how Elizabeth was managing the meeting.

It seemed to be going well, the conversation was staying light and superficial.

The nursemaids brought in the children, who climbed all over the ladies and he watched apprehensively to see whether Elizabeth would be all right. He was aware she had not slept very well the last few nights, but there seemed to be little he could do.

Mr. Gardiner commented on the fishing they had talked about at their last conversation here, and Mr. Darcy was forced to listen and make an appropriate rejoinder.

When he was next able to turn his attention back on his wife, the ladies were getting to their feet.

He stood quickly, concerned as to what was happening. Elizabeth smiled over at him, reassuringly. "We are going to stroll in the gardens and let the children run around."

The nursemaids were soon busy buttoning the children into their coats and the men waited in the hall for the ladies to be ready.

"I know you are concerned for Elizabeth," Mr. Gardiner said quietly. "Please do not be anxious, my wife is acutely conscious of the need to be as careful as is possible."

Mr. Darcy nodded silently. There was nothing to be said that would change anything, and they continued to make occasional conversation while they followed the ladies out to the gardens.

His mind was eased as they walked.

The children ran around, excited, while the nursemaids tried to marshal them to a smaller area. Georgiana helped the little girls to make daisy chains, laughing with them at their attempts.

Elizabeth and her aunt walked ahead, in earnest, quiet conversation. Mr. Darcy strolled behind with Mr. Gardiner.

"She is much better than she was," he said suddenly. "I am very hopeful that she will remember her past and trust other people more than she does at present. This visit is a first step for her, and I am most grateful that you have interrupted your lives to visit us."

"It is no hardship, sir." Mr. Gardiner was also watching the ladies in front of them. "As my wife said to you on our last visit, she was raised in Lambton and would like nothing better than to be able to live here while the children grow up." He sighed.

"It will not be possible, though, for some years."

"Is there anything I can do to help in that regard?" Mr. Darcy put his mind to the problem. "If you had a really good management team in London, I am sure a good estate could be found locally." His eyes rested on his wife, who seemed to be standing straighter, taller.

"I think it would be most beneficial to my wife to have her aunt living closer."

"You have invested a good deal into the family

already." Mr. Gardiner was in trade, and quite blunt about money. "I am sure Elizabeth does not remember, as I do, that it was your money that made it possible to ensure Lydia's ruin did not affect the family. Now you wish to —"

Darcy raised his hand. "To someone with my level of good fortune, the money is there to benefit others, quite as much as myself. If it would make your wife happy, and be better for the children while they are younger, then I pray that you consider the matter. But there is no need to intimate outside resources to anyone else."

CHAPTER 32

*E*lizabeth woke happy. She had to stop and think why she was particularly happy this day. Her husband's arm was resting across her, the warmth of his body and the weight of his arm were both comforting and his steady, even breathing was reassuring.

The sunlight was lancing in across the bed and she was surprised he was not awake and getting up.

Then she recalled that they had visitors. Dinner had continued very late as they talked and talked. Then, after the men had joined the ladies for coffee, they had talked again. It was just general conversation, but Elizabeth had been able to maintain her poise and hadn't felt a return of the overwhelming anxiety that had been concerning her. That was why she was happy.

And when they had retired for the night, she and Fitzwilliam had lain together in each other's arms and discussed the day. He told her he was so impressed and proud of her and the way she had managed to be a true hostess.

She had told him that she had talked about Gracechurch Street with her aunt and she had shared a few anecdotes from her stay which Elizabeth had been able to accept without becoming distressed that she didn't remember them.

"One day," she whispered to him. "One day, I'll know what I did that made you love me, and then I can keep doing it so that you never, never leave me."

He had held her close. "I will never, never leave you. Ever. You must not concern yourself with things that can never happen."

AFTER BREAKFAST, the two couples left for a visit to a local beauty spot. Georgiana said that she would stay and supervise the children until they returned. "I enjoyed playing with them yesterday."

Her brother laughed. "You will have to go to a

different part of the garden soon, or you will run out of daisies to make chains from."

Georgiana made a face at him. "We have many games to play, not just making daisy chains. When you are not watching me, I can be free to run with them."

Elizabeth saw her husband decide not to make any rejoinder, instead allowing his sister to have the final word.

As the weather was fair, they went in the open carriage, and Elizabeth spent much of the time enjoying the view. Her aunt didn't try and make conversation, but seemed to also enjoy the passing landscape.

When they arrived at the stopping place, the couples got out and looked up at the path as it climbed the moor.

"Well," said Mr. Gardiner. "I expect I will reach the summit just as you are ready to start down again." He laughed. "But I see there are benches at several points on the path. It is a most appropriate spot to have chosen."

"We will tell you what the view is like." His wife smiled sympathetically, and Elizabeth saw Mr. Darcy appear to be at somewhat of a dilemma. Should he stay close to his wife and protect her, or be a dutiful host and chat to the guest left behind?

She stepped towards him. "Aunt Gardiner and I will stay on the path, so we will always be within sight of you, sir. Thank you for the opportunity for me to meet her and talk. It is most helpful to me."

He acknowledged her comment with a small bow. "If you do not go fast, we will not be too far behind you."

She smiled and took her aunt's arm, and they began to pick their way slowly over the rough path. "I love the wild countryside so much. Was I the same when I was younger?"

"Oh, yes. Longbourn was very rural, I believe you were often out alone taking long walks in the hills and woodlands." Her aunt laughed. "I believe your mother tried a number of times to make you more ladylike, but she had to admit defeat. Your father encouraged you, he admired your independent spirit and your lively mind."

Elizabeth considered the information as she walked on in silence. "Are my sisters like me? Or was I lonely?"

"Your sisters are all very different," her aunt replied. "But I don't believe you were ever lonely. You were very close to your elder sister, Jane, but you also liked your own company. Sometimes I think you felt rather that you *could not* get away from being sociable, even if you wanted to be alone."

Elizabeth stopped and stared at her aunt. "I didn't know that about myself. I thought I must try and be an ordinary lady. I never heard of one who likes to be alone."

Her aunt smiled a little sadly. "Do you remember Longbourn at all? It was quite a small house for so many people to be living there — especially so many women. Your mother and some of your sisters could be quite — loud."

"I don't remember that," Elizabeth said softly, staring out at the hills. She had a lot to think about. No matter how she tried, she could not remember any of them. There was only the fleeting memory of Jane, that one memory.

And, of course, she had seen her youngest sister in Newcastle recently, but she shied from that. Of the others, there was nothing.

She hadn't felt the passing of time as she stood there, thinking of what her aunt had said about Longbourn, until her husband was beside her.

"Elizabeth, are you well?"

She started. "Oh!" she looked around. "I'm so sorry, I was just thinking. I didn't realise I would worry you."

He smiled. "It is quite all right. If you are well, then I am happy." He glanced at her aunt.

"Are you talking of old times?"

Elizabeth nodded. "It seems I enjoyed my own

company before this. I was anxious, because I cannot think of myself as a very sociable person, and I thought I must be so different from before."

He shook his head. "You are becoming like the old Elizabeth more and more. But you don't need to, unless it comes naturally. You are Elizabeth. Everyone changes as time goes on. You can be as you are. I will love you however you are."

She could feel herself blush as her face grew hot.

Her aunt tucked her arm into hers and tugged gently. "You have the ideal husband, Elizabeth. We will go on and try and reach the top before the men do."

CHAPTER 33

wo days later, Darcy was ready. He had reassured himself that Elizabeth would be safe here. She and her aunt had become confidantes again and Georgiana was also understanding. And Elizabeth herself seemed happier and more confident. He would be able to go to Newcastle.

He sat in the library, writing letters. One was to Colonel Batten, in command of Wickham's regiment, and another very brief note to Wickham. Then he went to the door and sent the footman to fetch his steward.

When Reed appeared, Darcy called him right in. "Mr. Reed, I am happy we have had these quieter weeks here at Pemberley. Do you feel yourself rested enough to take on another task?"

The man bowed. "Whatever you ask, sir."

"Good. I have to go back to Newcastle to pay Mr. Wickham the rest of the promised payment. I will not have him come to Pemberley. But I do not wish to be away from Mrs. Darcy too long, although I am assured she will be safe while Mr. and Mrs. Gardiner are here. I think I will be gone four days. I hope it will not be five."

The man bowed again.

"But I wish you to stay here, Reed. It is my view that Mrs. Darcy will be much safer with you here to ensure her security. I want you to make it your first concern when I am away. I will take Mr. James with me, as there is little to organise." He stopped to think.

"I will tell Mrs. Darcy and our guests about it tonight, at dinner. Please ensure the coach is ready to take me and Mr. James to meet the express post coach tomorrow at lunchtime." He thought. "I might even only be three nights away."

He gave the letters to Reed. "Meantime these need to go right away. Express."

The man bowed. "Yes, sir."

OVER DINNER THAT EVENING, Darcy rehearsed

the words in his mind. As they finished the meal, he sat forward.

"I am sorry to say I have a small matter of business which has called me away. I will need to leave tomorrow and go north, and I hope to be back within four or five days. I apologise for this neglect of my duties as host, but I am reassured that Elizabeth and Georgiana will not be alone here while you are our guests."

He smiled at his wife. "Elizabeth, I am satisfied that you will be safe here while I must be gone, and I hope you can forgive me for a few days neglect."

She smiled at him. "We ladies will have more time to talk about the things that interest us. Poor Uncle Gardiner will miss you the most."

Mr. Gardiner grunted. "Business is business. It cannot always wait for your convenience. We will await your return when you are done, Darcy."

He bowed to him. "Thank you, sir. I am indebted to you."

After the ladies had retired to the drawing room, he sat and talked to Mr. Gardiner until the niceties had been observed, and then they joined the ladies for an evening of music and conversation.

THE NEXT MORNING, he drew Mrs. Gardiner aside and explained why he had arranged to go while they were still guests. She patted his arm maternally.

"Do not concern yourself so, Mr. Darcy. There is nothing to worry about. I will ensure that we stay within the estate if it will make you happier."

He sighed. "That would be most satisfactory — if you are agreeable."

THREE NIGHTS LATER, the post coach stopped at an unimpressive little backstreet inn in York. Darcy was tired and irritable. He'd had to allow himself to be entertained by Colonel Patten and that had wasted hours of his time. But he hadn't wanted to cause any possible offence, and he was pleased that he had exerted himself to be pleasant when the man bowed to him at the door as he left.

"I am glad your business was concluded satisfactorily, Darcy. I will undertake to keep you informed of any interesting information pertaining to Wickham, if you wish."

That might be useful. "Sir, I would be exceedingly grateful." Darcy bowed in return, and the colonel laughed.

"I'm glad you have told me of the payment you have made to him. I will ensure his mess bill is presented to him early tomorrow morning."

Mr. Darcy smiled to himself as he walked into the inn. He was sure Wickham had by now been relieved of most of the money to pay debts. Mrs. Wickham would be most disagreeable if she could not buy a new hat.

He sat down to dinner. Mr. James appeared by his table.

"There is a letter waiting for you, sir."

Darcy took the letter, recognising Mrs.Gardiner's handwriting. He frowned. He had of course, informed her of the route and proposed stops in case of need, but hadn't expected to hear from anyone. He broke the seal hastily.

> *Dear Mr. Darcy*
>
> *I have been in some difficulty to decide*
> *whether to write to you or not,*
> *because I already know you are*
> *travelling as fast as you can, so there*
> *might be nothing you can do to get*
> *here any sooner, but I think that you*
> *would want to know we have had*
> *trouble here, and it will be well when*
> *you can get home.*
>
> *First of all, to reassure you, Elizabeth is*

here, and she is safe now, but she has been most shocked and frightened by events and I think she needs your presence very much.

Your man, Mr. Reed, has been seen by the physician, who assures us that he will recover, but he has received a deep knife wound to his arm while trying to protect Elizabeth.

Darcy leapt to his feet, dinner quite forgotten.

"Mr. James! Hold the express post coach! It must not go. Get our belongings back on there immediately and pay off the rooms we have booked. We are going on at once." He turned back to his letter.

It appears that he recognised the man who had previously attempted to abduct Elizabeth in a team of men delivering items to the gardeners here. We have since discovered that he had access to money to pay the guards for him to escape prison, and had made his way south.

Mr. Darcy's lips tightened.

*I think that he has a wish for revenge, to
take Elizabeth and do her serious
harm. If he could not take her, he
was prepared to kill her to punish you
and your steward.*

*We were walking in the gardens together
when this man ran from the group
with two accomplices, and snatched
her. They were able to drag her some
way towards the entrance when Mr.
Reed reached them, and he
immediately began a struggle in her
defence.*

*Once he had engaged them, other staff
joined him and soon Elizabeth was
able to pull herself free, receiving only
a small cut from the knife.*

Darcy's heart twisted in agony at the anguish
she must have suffered, and still be suffering.

*But she has been most grievously
distressed. Mr. Reed called out to her
to run and enter the house, which she
did. The physician has attended to
her, and dressed her wound, but her
emotions have been much affected.
We have been unable to persuade her*

*from your bedchamber, where she
insists on staying, and she has been
most anxious.*

*I have been able to persuade her to take a
little soup, but I think she will be
much relieved when you have
returned home.*

*I am sorry to have to send the news while
you are far from home, and I must
caution you not to take any risk of
accident by way of attempting to
accelerate your journey. It is most
important that you arrive safely.*

He agreed with those sentiments, and he would most certainly arrive before any letter could. He hastily pushed her letter in his pocket and hurried out to the coach, leaving his dinner utterly forgotten.

"You!" he accosted the coachman. "Will there be a coach to hire at Sheffield for an urgent journey? I must get to my estate near Bakewell."

The man nodded. "Yes, sir. Someone will be available at the post stop, although they might need half an hour to ready the horses."

"Thank you. I am grateful." Darcy looked around for his manservant and saw him waiting beside the coach.

"I am sorry at the change of plans, Mr. James. Is all the luggage aboard?"

"Yes, sir."

"Then we must go." He swung himself up into the coach, where the passenger who had been made to wait while the luggage was reloaded glowered at him. Darcy did not have time to make pleasantries and stared out into the darkness. He tried to remember the contents of the letter, it was too dark to reread it.

Elizabeth had a small knife wound — had the letter said where it was? He couldn't recall that. But he was far more concerned about her state of mind. His heart broke at the thought of her being alone without him.

Sixty miles. Sixty miles to Sheffield. Then a delay while he found a coach to take him as fast as possible for the final twenty miles. He could not possibly be there before the middle of the day. He almost groaned in anger at the slowness of the journey, and sat back, willing it to pass as fast as possible.

Elizabeth. He must reach her soon.

CHAPTER 34

She lay, curled up tightly, in her husband's bed, watching as the dawn again sent slivers of sunlight across the room. Surely he would be home soon? She must have been here for days now. His bed gave her comfort, and she held beside her face the nightshirt he had worn, the smell of him a solace that he would return.

How had Fuller known she was here? Had he been watching until her husband went away? How did he know to strike for her the very day he had gone?

She let the tears flow. Now she would never be free of the fear of him finding her, taking her, using her and killing her. She would never know the joy of a long and happy marriage, the gift of children, without being afraid of him.

He had pulled her close to him, his arm pressed against her bosom, his foul breath hissing across her throat. "You're a proud one, m'lady. Think yourself above the likes of me, I reckon. But you are mine. I marked you down as mine the night we took you. I will use you how I like and make your man regret he ever looked away for a moment." He'd laughed, coarse and lecherous, and her heart had frozen in fear.

Her poor, poor Fitzwilliam! How he would punish himself. But it wasn't his fault, he had taken such care of her. She struggled back.

"Let me go, you monster!" And she tried to stamp back onto his foot. His arm had tightened then around her neck and he had dragged her backwards, leaving her scrambling to keep her footing. Her vision had blurred, faded, seeing the horrified faces of the ladies; Aunt Gardiner pulling Georgiana back as another man threatened them with a knife.

Why had they walked out here without a gentleman, or staff? Why had they taken such a risk, and how had Fuller and the others got into the estate?

Then she had been saved, again by Mr. Reed. She owed him so much. He had attacked Fuller without a second thought, to protect her, his master's wife. And the other gardeners, who had been standing helpless, had rushed in too. Seeing hope, she had struggled again. A sharp pain across the back of her hand, and she was free, staggering to regain her feet.

"Run back to the house, Mrs. Darcy. Run!" Reed's voice had caught her attention and she'd obeyed without a second thought, but had turned within a couple of paces. The men had knives, she couldn't leave Reed to fight and get killed for her.

"No, madam, go! I cannot protect you otherwise!" he'd shouted, and she'd stared, helpless, for just a moment, before turning back to the house.

Mrs. Reynolds had met her in the hall, a large linen cloth in her hands and she'd tried to bind Elizabeth's bleeding hand. But she had stared at the housekeeper in fear, trying to think, to stay calm, to remember who she was and her mind teetered again.

Mr. Fuller was here. Was Papa here? Did he need help again? But she had been tired, so very tired and she wasn't Sarah. She didn't know who she was, but she wasn't Sarah.

She had known safety was upstairs, though, and she'd run along the corridors until she'd found a door that was right. In there, she'd calmed a little, smelling the calm, comforting familiar smell of the tall, dark man who was her whole life. Was he only in her dreams?

There she'd stayed, the one place she felt safe. It hadn't been long before there had been a knock on the door and the woman had entered, an elegant lady. She'd been outside there, where Fuller had … No, she mustn't think of that. There was a man with her and she had cringed away from him.

"Elizabeth." The woman had spoken. "The physician is here to dress your wound. Then we can leave you until you feel better." She'd approached with a gentle smile.

"You're safe now. Let the physician see your hand, and then we can make you feel better." Her voice was calm, cajoling, as if she was speaking to a small child, and she — Sarah? Elizabeth? — felt embarrassed now.

She held out her hand and let the man examine it, pronounce it needed only bandaging and let him do that.

Then he looked at her kindly, and turned to the other lady. "Let her stay here if it comforts her. She must drink and eat very nourishing foods until she is well again."

She had stayed pressed with her back against the wall the whole time, but when they had left the room she had scrambled across to his bed and burrowed into it.

Where was he? She remembered his name.

Mr. Darcy. He must have a given name, but her mind seemed to be fading. She lay, terrified, and the room seemed to go black.

Now a few days had passed. She must be strong, she must get up today, or the bed would lose the smell of him. Already it smelled more like her, and less and less like him.

She looked around her carefully. She was alone. She crept out of bed and along the wall to the closet and slipped inside. Here, the smell of him was much stronger, and she buried her face in his shirts.

"Elizabeth!" the voice was panicked. It was the kind-faced lady, and Elizabeth — she must be Elizabeth, that was what everyone called her — looked out of the closet, still with an armful of shirts.

The lady smiled in relief. "There you are. I suppose his clothes are comforting with the scent."

Elizabeth just nodded.

"That is good. Why not bring them out with you? I have some tea here for you, and some coddled eggs. You must keep your strength up. I am sure Mr. Darcy will be home in a day or two, and he will be most pleased if you have eaten something."

She sat beside Elizabeth and encouraged her to eat. She didn't try and get her to talk, but having her eat something seemed to please her, and after a while she took the tray away.

She climbed into the bed again, his shirts still clutched in her arms, and drifted off to sleep.

WHEN SHE WOKE, she sensed his presence. He was there, kneeling beside the bed, his hand on hers. Her eyes flew open and she saw her beloved husband. She noticed in one instant that he looked exhausted, dishevelled, and tormented, but she didn't allow herself a moment to take any of it in, but scrambled out of the bed and threw herself into his arms.

"You're here, you're here, you came back."

CHAPTER 35

*D*arcy gathered her into his arms and held her close. This was what he had wanted to do, all those endless hours on the coach.

Indeed, when he'd hurried into the house twenty minutes ago, he'd headed straight for the stairs, but Mrs. Gardiner had stood in his way.

"Mr. Darcy, go and see Mr. Reed first. I have just been upstairs and Elizabeth is asleep. Once you're with her, you will not want to leave her and you should see Mr. Reed today. If it was not for his bravery, you might no longer have Elizabeth."

He had seen the sense in that, and had tried not to scowl. He turned and reluctantly headed to the servant's quarters to go to Reed's rooms. The steward and the housekeeper each had the best of the staff quarters, and it was well-deserved, Darcy could not run the estate without them.

He sent Mr. James down ahead, seeking permission to visit the steward, and found him sitting up, looking rather sheepish.

"I am sorry, sir. I should be back at work very soon."

Mr. Darcy broke with tradition and shook his hand very earnestly. "I will have no more of that. I owe you more than I can say. You protected my wife, putting your own life at risk for her. I am forever in your debt. Again."

They sat down and chatted idly for a few moments. "I hope you will excuse me for the rest of the day," he'd said eventually. "I wish to go and see Mrs. Darcy now. But I will visit you again tomorrow. I am most pleased to see there is no sign of an infection, and I hope you will make a good recovery."

"I'm honoured by your presence, sir. That you came to see me before Mrs. Darcy — well, I am humbled." Mr. Reed bowed respectfully, and Darcy felt a little ashamed.

But he'd put that out of his mind as he hurried up the stairs to his rooms.

He entered silently, and saw the disorder that would have caused him to become exceedingly displeased only a few months ago. But now he had eyes only for the sleeping figure of his wife, curled up into a small, defensive ball, clutching at a bundle of his clothing for the comfort of him.

His heart swelled with emotion and he had knelt beside her, noting the bandage around her wrist, and her tear-stained face. He placed one hand on hers, needing so much to touch her. He just watched for a few moments as she slept. Then he saw her stir, and her eyes flew open. That was when she had thrown herself into his arms.

HE PICKED her up and went over to the chair and sat with her on his lap, feeling his heart thundering in his chest as she pushed herself closer.

"I'm sorry, I'm so sorry," she murmured jerkily.

"There is nothing to be sorry about. Nothing at all. I'm so happy that you're here and safe."

They sat in silence for many minutes. He wanted her to know that he was back with her, and he needed to hold her close for a long time to assure himself she was real and she was still really here.

He could so easily have lost her again, so easily

have lost her forever. As they sat there, he found himself going over the steps to make her utterly safe. He would get more staff, throw such a ring around the estate, that no one who wished her harm would get past.

And he would deal with Fuller. The man was now in local custody. He would go and see the magistrate, make sure that he was allowed no visitors or letters to gain access to money to bribe anyone. There were enough staff to testify on the assault and the injury to Reed to get a conviction, but just the escape from jail in Northumberland was enough for him to be deported, or even to hang.

But Darcy needed to know, needed to be able to assure Elizabeth in the future that she would never see him again. So he would see the magistrate and make sure he heard of the sentence. He would make sure he saw the man loaded on to the transport or hanged. He must be sure Fuller did not escape justice again.

Elizabeth cringed and looked up. "What is it, sir?"

He shook his head, bemused. "What do you mean?"

"You are concerned, sir. You're thinking angry thoughts."

He forced himself to relax. "It was just anger

at myself, that I wasn't here to protect you, Elizabeth. I am so sorry about that." He must remember how sensitive she was to his emotions, so much more than anyone else.

He smiled. "Do you remember my name? Then you won't have to call me *sir*."

She sighed happily. "I remember now — Fitzwilliam. But I nearly couldn't, when I saw … saw him." Her voice trembled.

"Mr. Reed said to run for the house and I came up here, but all I could think about was Fuller and then I thought Papa must be here and then this lady came in and I didn't know who she was." Elizabeth drooped unhappily. "I couldn't remember anything, except I knew about you. If I waited here, I knew you might find me again."

"I'm so happy to be back here with you, Elizabeth. And I am pleased that you could come to my rooms and that they gave you comfort."

She sat herself up, and her hands went to her hair. Her face was a picture of horror. "Sir — Fitzwilliam, I am sorry, I am so dishevelled I must look most unseemly." She tried to get out of his grasp and he instinctively wanted to hold her. But he must not make her feel trapped. He loosened his grasp.

"You are beautiful. I think you and I would both feel better if we freshened up." He drew his hand across his unshaven jaw. Then he stood up and drew her to him.

"I told you before that you were safe here. I made a terrible mistake, for which I can only hope you will forgive me." His arms were around her, he never wished to let her go. "But inside this house, you are safe. We could bathe and then meet here again, if you feel able to do that?"

She took a deep breath and nodded. "I am more confident now you are here. I felt my whole world rock, I forget almost who I was, all over again. But now you are here, I am finding those things are still here, I can recall them again."

She looked inward. "Poor Aunt Gardiner. I must have frightened her very much. But now I know who she is again."

"You had a most distressing and terrible experience. But you are my own strong and independent Elizabeth. I know that you'll get over this and I know that we will always be together."

She nodded and smiled up at him. But the smile had sadness behind it, and he tipped her face up towards him. "I will make sure you never, never, see that odious man again, Elizabeth. I will make sure you are always safe."

She lifted her hand and her fingers traced the line of his jaw. "I am most fortunate to be your wife. Thank you for protecting me."

She smiled again. "And … and I like it when you're unshaven, it makes my heart race."

He looked down at her, his finger tracing her lips.

"My dearest Elizabeth."

CHAPTER 36

*I*t was an hour later when she descended the stairs, her arm in her husband's. But still she needed to grasp the bannister rail tightly.

"Are you well, Elizabeth?" His head dipped toward her. "You may stay upstairs if you would be happier."

She shook her head. "I must do this. And I can, now that you're with me."

Aunt Gardiner hurried out of the drawing room into the hall. "Elizabeth! It is good to see you looking so much better." But she was sensitive to Elizabeth and did not come close to her.

But Elizabeth felt much better now. With her husband beside her, she felt invincible. "Aunt Gardiner, thank you for your concerns. I'm so sorry I could not recall who you were and what was happening to me. But now I remember, and Mr. Darcy tells me it was your letter that brought him home today instead of tomorrow. So I am much indebted to you several times over."

They went into the drawing room and Georgiana rang for tea. She glanced at Elizabeth, but did not speak.

Elizabeth racked her mind to think of something to say. "Thank you, Georgiana, for entertaining my aunt and uncle while I have been indisposed. I'm most grateful to you."

"I'm just glad you're feeling better, Elizabeth." And the conversations moved on away from the incident.

Sitting on the sofa next to her husband, Elizabeth noted that he didn't join in the conversations very much, and as she watched him, she saw the fatigue soaking out of him. His features were gaunt, and he was grey with exhaustion.

Now that he was home, he could relax and she wanted to relieve him of any responsibilities until he was more rested. But she was sure he would not shirk his duty as host.

"Mr. Darcy, I wonder if I may ask for dinner to be bought forward somewhat. It would enable you to rest earlier. You look most fatigued."

He smiled lazily at her, then forced himself to

sit up. "I am being a dilatory host, I must apologise most sincerely."

"It is unnecessary." Georgiana leaned forward. "I have already instructed that dinner be served early, we will all be tired after the emotions of the day." She turned to Elizabeth. "Shall I play a little? Then all you need to do is listen."

Elizabeth looked around at her husband, who nodded slightly.

She nodded back and turned to her sister-in-law. "That is an excellent plan, thank you."

She was very conscious of his presence as she sat beside him. He would not act in a way that would upset his guests, but he was sitting closer than was usual in public, and he had contrived that the side of his thigh, strong and hard, was resting against hers. He would know instantly if she moved — or was taken — away from him. She shivered a little at the thought and he turned towards her at once.

"Are you well?" his murmur was low and she didn't think anyone was aware of his voice.

"I am here." She tried to smile reassuringly. It would take a long time for both of them to recover from this. "I never want to be more than an arm's distance away from you again."

He contemplated his arm. "Your arm's length. It is shorter than mine." His eyes met hers. "We will beat this. I know it will take time, and it does not matter how long. But we will do this, Elizabeth. You and I, and as much of your past life as you care for and enjoy."

She felt her eyes fill, she was so fortunate that this man loved her. She couldn't speak, she just nodded.

When she looked away, she saw Aunt Gardiner watching and felt her own cheeks grow hot.

But her aunt was smiling gently as they listened to Georgiana playing on the pianoforte, and as the moment passed, Elizabeth was conscious of little else than his comforting presence beside her.

All through dinner, she was conscious of him and she longed for the day to end so that they were once again alone together upstairs. She would not need to hold his garments close, for he himself would be there and she wished for nothing else than to be in his arms.

CHAPTER 37

Epilogue

Six months had passed and at last she felt that her healing was secure and she felt sure of herself. Although some parts of her past were empty, it no longer distressed her.

Elizabeth moved to the window. She was up in her bedchamber, right next to her husband's, and the windows looked out over the parkland of the estate. But it was possible to see the long private drive as it curved through the landscape, and along which a heavy coach was arriving, drawn by four handsome matched chestnut horses.

She felt a shiver of excitement going through

her. It had been a long half year of slow recovery and gaining confidence. She had been in extensive correspondence and now the time was nearly here.

She hurried back to the glass and checked her appearance, smoothing down her gown.

She looked up at the knock on the connecting door from her husband's rooms, and he opened it and came through. He bowed.

"You look most beautiful, my dear Elizabeth, and I'm sure you have seen the coach approaching."

"Yes, Fitzwilliam." She went up to him and dipped a curtsey to him before taking the hand he held out to her. "I am both eager and anxious to meet them at last."

He lifted her hand to his lips. "I am beside you, there is nothing to fear." His eyes searched her face. "Mr. and Mrs. Bingley will be as anxious as you are, I'm sure."

She nodded. "Should I greet her as Jane, or as Mrs. Bingley? Which would be correct?"

He drew her into his arms. "You have been corresponding for many months now, and you are recalling more and more of your childhood together. I would think greeting her as Jane is perfectly in order, if you are comfortable doing that."

She sighed happily. "Thank you."

He turned for the door. "It is time to greet them. We have as much time as we need to rekindle your relationship with her."

She hesitated slightly. "Wait. Is Mr. Bingley's sister with them? I recall she did not like me very much."

He drew her towards the door again. "She is staying with her sister in London, I believe. It is just your sister and her husband who have come to be our guests."

"I am grateful to you. I am sure you had something to do with that."

They began to descend the sweeping staircase. He chuckled. "I do not deny it. I will be happy to see my friend and not have to ward off the attentions of Miss Bingley."

They waited at the bottom of the steps outside the house as the coach door was opened and the steps lowered. Mr. Bingley got out first and turned to give his hand to his lady and assist her.

Elizabeth watched his face, trying to commit it to her memory. She had to learn new faces carefully now and was determined that she never fail. His face was open, honest and good-humoured. She smiled, her sister must be happy.

Then she looked at Jane, and knew that the

snippet of memory she'd had was accurate. Jane was beautiful.

She glanced anxiously at Elizabeth, but Elizabeth didn't hesitate. She ran forward and embraced her sister. "Oh, Jane! How happy I am to see you! Thank you for your patience and forbearance while we corresponded."

Jane's arms were around her too, the first person other than her husband to hold her close since that man tried to drag her away. No. She pushed that thought from her mind, and stepped back.

"I had a picture in my mind of how you look, Jane, and I was wrong. You are far more beautiful than I remember."

Her husband was watching her closely. She smiled at him, she could do this. She approached Mr. Bingley and curtsied. "Welcome to Pemberley, Mr. Bingley."

He bowed. "Delighted, Mrs. Darcy, delighted." He glanced anxiously at his friend, and Elizabeth turned and tucked her arm inside her sister's.

"Come and have some tea, Jane."

Jane looked around her as they climbed the steps. "What a beautiful place, Lizzy. I will look forward to you showing me around." She looked concerned as Elizabeth hesitated. "I'm sorry, did I say something wrong?"

"Oh, no." She hastened to reassure her. "It's just that I am not used to hearing the name Lizzy any more. I have to get used to it, and I will."

Jane squeezed her arm. "You must tell me how I must behave and what I should say. I have to confess I have been anxious about coming. It seems so very long since we have seen each other, and so much has happened to you. I do not wish to cause you any more trouble or unhappiness."

"And you will not." Elizabeth was determined to ease her sister's mind. "You know the story, so I do not have to relive it by telling you. All I want is for us to be friends again, and I want to hear that you are happily married and that your life is all you hoped it could be."

"That I can assure you of right now." Jane smiled contentedly. "Mr. Bingley has been amiability itself. He is most obliging and spends all his time in trying to please me."

"I'm so happy to hear that." Elizabeth led her into the drawing room. "May I introduce you to Miss Georgiana Darcy?"

The two ladies greeted each other and the gentlemen followed them into the room. Elizabeth had been conscious of her husband's attention as the guests arrived and she felt secure that he would intervene if she had any difficulty. That made things very easy for her and she could relax, get to know Jane and hear about the family she still had no desire to know more closely.

As she sat next to her sister for tea, she looked over at the gentlemen, who were deep in conversation, standing by the window. Mr. Darcy looked up, and their eyes met.

He loved her, the whole story was in his gaze. She was safe, she was home with the man of her dreams, the man who had saved her. She need never fear anything again.